I crouched down to get a better look at some of the titles on the bottom shelf. At that moment there was another soft thud from the next room, but this time I forced myself not to jump like a silly schoolgirl. Instead I ran my fingers lightly across the spines of the books on the shelf, ignoring the sound.

As my finger stopped on a book about pythons, I heard another, louder thud directly behind me, followed by another noise, also much closer than the next room. The latter was a quieter but much more unsettling sound, sort of like a dry pinecone clattering along the ground. I turned my head—and froze in terror.

Just two or three feet behind me, its head raised to strike, was an enormous rattlesnake!

NANCY DREW
girl detective™

Available from Aladdin Paperbacks

This book belongs to:

NANCY DREW
girl detective ™

#18

Pit of Vipers

CAROLYN KEENE

Aladdin Paperbacks
New York London Toronto Sydney

This book is a work of fiction. Any references to historical events, real people, or real locales are used fictitiously. Other names, characters, places, and incidents are the product of the author's imagination, and any resemblance to actual events or locales or persons, living or dead, is entirely coincidental.

❧ALADDIN PAPERBACKS
An imprint of Simon & Schuster Children's Publishing Division
1230 Avenue of the Americas, New York, NY 10020
Copyright © 2006 by Simon & Schuster, Inc.
All rights reserved, including the right of
reproduction in whole or in part in any form.
NANCY DREW is a registered trademark of Simon & Schuster, Inc.
ALADDIN PAPERBACKS, NANCY DREW: GIRL DETECTIVE, and
colophon are trademarks of Simon & Schuster, Inc.
Manufactured in the United States of America
First Aladdin Paperbacks edition July 2006
10 9 8 7 6 5 4 3
Library of Congress Control Number 2006922048
ISBN-13: 978-1-4169-1180-7
ISBN-10: 1-4169-1180-4

Contents

Pit of Vipers

1

Car Trouble

Look out, Nancy!"

George Fayne's terrified shriek made me jump, and I almost steered my car straight into a parked pickup truck I was passing. "What?" I exclaimed, shooting my friend an exasperated glance. "What's the matter?"

"You almost sideswiped those cars," Bess Marvin complained, leaning forward from the backseat to glare at me. Bess was George's cousin and my other best friend. Normally she's a pretty easygoing type of person, but at the moment she was anything but. "Kind of a close call, wasn't it?" she added.

For some reason, my friends get nervous whenever they ride with me. I'm not sure why—I really don't drive any faster than they do, and my cute little hybrid car steers and brakes quite well. They like to claim that I'm too easily distracted. But that's not really true. I just believe in multitasking—not only can I walk and chew gum at the same time, but I can even drive while I talk or think. What's the big deal?

"If you guys would just relax and enjoy the ride, maybe I wouldn't have so many close calls," I said mildly. To mollify them, though, I slowed down slightly as I approached the next turn.

"Maybe if you didn't drive like a crazed howler monkey in a NASCAR race, we *could* relax," George countered, running a hand through her short-cropped dark hair. "Riding a condemned roller coaster is more relaxing."

"I told you we shouldn't have let her drive," Bess grumbled from the backseat.

I eased to a halt at the stop sign at the corner of Bluff Street. "Whoa," I said, giving my friends a look. "You didn't have much choice, remember? George's parents asked us to pick up Scott, and neither of you has a functioning car at your disposal at the moment. So cool it!"

George and Bess both shifted in their seats, making me think I'd been heard. "Besides," I added, "we're almost there, and we're all still in one piece." I glanced at the digital clock in the dashboard. "And we're right on schedule—we're only about a mile from the pool, so we should get there just in time for Scott's swim team practice to finish."

"Great," George mumbled as I hit the gas again. "The only thing that sounds like more fun than riding in a car with Daredevil Drew at the wheel is adding my moody little brother as a fellow passenger."

Bess shot her cousin a sympathetic glance. "So Scott's still acting like a creature from another planet today?"

"Big time." George blew out a noisy sigh. "This morning at breakfast he just about snapped my head off when I asked him to pass the butter. He's been like that all week, and it's getting old fast. I was just about to ask Nancy to solve the mystery of who suddenly switched Scott's personality with a rabid badger."

I grinned. Everyone who knows me knows there's nothing I love more than a good mystery. I've been tracking down clues and solving stubborn puzzles for just about as long as I can remember.

"We don't need Nancy to solve this one," Bess told George with a chuckle. "I can give you the answer right now. Scott's twelve, remember? He's finally on his way to becoming an honest-to-goodness teenager."

"Don't laugh too hard, Bess," George warned with a frown. "Your dear little sister Maggie is twelve too, remember? It'll be your turn soon—and I'm sure you'll love the obnoxious comments, the cranky moods, the constant arguing . . ."

"And don't forget the if-looks-could-kill glares," I added, glancing over at them. "Scott shot me one of those yesterday when I complimented the T-shirt he was wearing."

Bess laughed. "Okay, okay," she said. "You guys have a point. I guess I shouldn't—whoa, look out!"

My eyes veered immediately back to the road. There were no other cars in sight for at least a block, and for a split second I wasn't sure why Bess was gasping and pointing ahead.

Then I saw the giant pothole looming right in front of the car.

"Oops!" I blurted out, spinning the wheel.

Too little, too late. I felt my right front tire hit the jagged edge of the hole and bounce sickeningly up and to one side. The whole car lurched, and there was an unpleasant-sounding *crunch* and *pop* from somewhere in the vicinity of the front end.

"Oooh," George said as I jammed on the brakes. "That didn't sound good."

I threw the car into park and climbed out, hurrying around to the front to see the damage. The right tire looked like a squashed donut. Even from several feet away, it was easy to spot the ragged laceration showing where the tire had struck the edge of the pothole and blown out.

Bess and George got out to look too. "Nice going, Mario Andretti," George said. "So much for being on time to pick up Scott."

"No big deal." Bess was already heading for the back of the car. Fortunately for us, she's just as handy with a tire iron as she is with a mascara wand. "We'll just pop on the spare. That should hold us long enough to get Scott home."

I gulped as she popped open the trunk. "Um, Bess?"

"Hey, where's your spare?"

"That's what I was about to tell you. I'm, uh . . . already driving on it." I gestured to the right rear tire. "I ran over a nail or something last week and Ned and I had to change it, and I didn't quite get around to taking it in for a new tire yet."

Bess's head popped into view around the sloping back end of the car. "Oh, Nancy!" she cried as sorrowfully as if I'd just told her my spare tire was missing because I'd been using it to club orphan puppies over the head.

I reached into my pocket, searching for my cell phone. "Don't worry," I said. "I'll call the garage—I'm sure they can be out here with a new tire in a jiffy."

George's expression changed instantly from irritation to amusement. "Yeah. Especially if Charlie Adams is on duty. When he hears it's Nancy calling, he'll drop everything. Bad brakes? Transmission trouble? Never mind, it can wait—Nancy Drew needs a tire!"

I rolled my eyes as Bess giggled. Charlie Adams works for a local garage. He's just a few years older than me and has always been a good friend—he doesn't even charge me half the time when he comes to tow me out of my latest round of car trouble. Okay, and maybe there's some circumstantial evidence that he might have the teeniest, tiniest crush on me. However, there's even better evidence that my friends tend to exaggerate his feelings.

"Very funny," I said. "You'd better watch what you say, or I'll tell him to leave you both here by the side of the road. Now, where's my stupid phone. . . ."

Before I could go back to the car in search of my missing cell, George pulled hers out of her pocket and tossed it to me. "Here," she said. "Use mine. And hurry." She glanced at her watch. "Because unless good ol' Chuck has developed the ability to turn back time, we're still going to be late."

"Not that late," Bess said soothingly. "It doesn't take long to change a tire, and we can call the pool to let Scott know we're still coming."

"No, we can't," George fretted. "There's never anybody in the office there during practices. And with the way Scott's been acting lately, he'll probably give up after waiting thirty seconds and decide to hitch-hike to Chicago or something."

I dialed the all-too-familiar number for Carr's Garage and put George's phone to my ear as the line started ringing. Soon someone picked up at the other end.

"Carr's Garage," a young man's voice said.

"Charlie? Hi, it's Nancy."

"Uh, this isn't Charlie. It's Lionel Hart. Can I help you?"

"Oops, sorry about that. I thought you were . . . um, this is Nancy Drew. I'm hoping you can help me out. . . ."

Soon Lionel Hart had taken down my location. He promised to head out right away with the tow truck and bring my car back to the garage, so the mechanics could check it over while they put on two new tires.

"There," I said with satisfaction, hanging up the phone and handing it back to George. Realizing that my car was still on, I leaned in through the driver's side door and punched the button on the dashboard to turn off the engine. "Now all we have to do is wait."

"But what about Scott?" George said worriedly.

"He'll have no idea where we are. Seriously, if he thinks we forgot him, he's liable to take offense and report us to the police for neglect or something."

"Chief McGinnis would just *love* that," Bess commented, shooting me an amused look. The River Heights police chief doesn't have the highest opinion of me, mostly due to all the times I've accidentally made him look bad by solving his cases for him. I always do my best to share the credit with him when possible, but I think he probably still wishes I'd move to another city—or at least give up the detective work!

At the moment, though, the only mystery on my mind was the one involving how we were going to get to the River Heights Swim Club within the next ten minutes.

As I glanced around for ideas, my gaze fell on the bus stop sign half a block away. "I've got it," I said. "George, why don't you hop the next bus over to the pool and pick up Scott. Then you two can take the bus to the garage and meet us. By the time you get there, the car should be ready to go."

"Take the bus?" George said dubiously, glancing toward the bus stop.

"Sure," I said. "Look, I think I see one coming now."

Sure enough, a city bus was lumbering down the

street a couple of blocks up. River Heights isn't big enough to have much in the way of public transportation, but one thing it does have is a fairly convenient and reliable, albeit small, public bus fleet.

"Go ahead." Bess gave her cousin a gentle push in the direction of the bus stop. "I'll stay here and keep Nancy out of trouble." She glanced at the blown tire. "Any *more* trouble, I mean."

George stuck her hands in her pockets. "I don't think I have enough for the fare."

Bess and I exchanged a glance and a sigh. George spends money as fast as she gets it—mainly because she never met an electronic gadget she didn't desperately covet. She's almost always short of cash when, say, it's time to divvy up the check after lunch at a restaurant or when we reach the ticket counter at the movie theater.

"I've got you covered." I reached into the car's center well, where I keep a bunch of change for parking meters and such. Grabbing a handful of coins, I shoved it at her. "Now hurry, or you'll miss it."

George pocketed the money and sprinted for the bus stop. Bess and I watched until she was safely on board, then wandered over to wait for the tow truck on the bench in front of a small bakery.

"So is Scott really that bad?" I asked her, leaning back and taking in a deep breath of pastry-scented air. "I haven't seen him that much lately."

"He's pretty bad," Bess said. "But I think the worst thing is that it happened so suddenly. Less than two weeks ago he was this great kid, and now he's a snarling stranger half the time. It's weird." She shrugged. "But I guess that's how it happens sometimes."

"I guess." As an only child, I could only imagine what it would be like to have a sibling change like that. "Maybe it's just a passing mood."

"Maybe." Bess didn't sound too hopeful. "It's just a shame he's so grumpy when he has so much going for him these days. He got fantastic grades in school last year, he has tons of friends, he's the star of his swim team—thanks to him they qualified for some huge regional meet, which I think is in a couple of days, come to think of it—and he's got a cushy part-time job walking dogs in the neighborhood."

"Yeah, but he still has one very serious problem that could bring anybody down," I said somberly.

"What?"

I grinned. "He's still stuck being George's little brother."

That lightened the mood, and our conversation turned to other topics. Finally we heard the roar of a diesel engine at the end of the block, and we looked up to see the familiar green and white shape of the Carr's tow truck trundling toward us.

I jumped to my feet and hurried forward as the truck swung in and positioned itself in front of my car. A moment later a clean-cut young man hopped out of the cab.

"Hi, there," he called, squinting at us in the bright afternoon sunlight. "One of you Nancy Drew?" He smiled hopefully at Bess, who looked as gorgeous as always in her powder blue sundress.

Hiding a grin at his look of open admiration—which, true to form, Bess appeared not to notice—I lifted my hand. "That's me," I told him. "I'm Nancy. Are you Lionel?"

"Yep." He turned his attention to me, then glanced at the car. "Looks like you really did a number on that tire."

Bess giggled, and I nodded ruefully. "Yeah," I said. "You don't think I bent the axle or anything, do you?"

"We'll take a look back at the shop, just in case," he assured me. "Now let's get you hooked up and out of here."

"Sure," I said. "Thanks. Hey, I almost forgot to ask—where's Charlie today? Is it his day off or something?"

Lionel shot me a surprised look. Then he frowned. "You mean Charlie Adams? Uh, I dunno if I'm supposed to say anything to customers," he mumbled uncertainly. "But since you asked specifically, I guess it's okay. . . ."

"What?" I was really curious now. "He didn't quit, did he?"

Lionel shook his head and ran one grease-stained hand through his short blond hair. "Nope," he said sadly. "Charlie came to work as usual this morning. But Chief McGinnis himself came by the shop 'bout an hour ago and arrested him."

A Duo of Disappearances

My jaw dropped. "Charlie—arrested?" I cried. "For what?"

Lionel shrugged. "Dunno. The chief didn't seem to be in a chatty mood. He just dragged Charlie off with him—for questioning, I think he said. Excuse me, it'll just take me a minute to get your car hooked up. . . ."

As Lionel hurried off to do his thing, I exchanged a glance with Bess. She looked as surprised and puzzled as I felt. Charlie wasn't the type to get in trouble with the law—far from it. As far as I knew, he didn't drink, gamble, or even jaywalk.

"Weird," Bess said, succinctly summing up my own thoughts. "I wonder what that's all about."

"I don't know," I said. "But I plan to find out.

Someone at the garage might know more than Lionel does—or at least be willing to share it."

As I wandered over to see how Lionel was coming along, I spotted my cell phone in the backseat. Reaching in, I grabbed it and stuck it in my pocket.

"Almost ready to go?" I asked Lionel, trying not to let my impatience show.

"Just about."

He was right. It was only a few more minutes before my car was hooked to the back of the tow truck, and Bess and I were crammed into the seat beside Lionel. The truck's cab smelled like a combination of axle grease and peanuts, a scent I realized I always associated with Charlie. Then again, I associated the entire cab of that truck with Charlie—it was kind of weird looking across Bess and seeing a stranger sitting at the wheel.

"Thanks for coming out so quickly, Lionel," I said as he pulled out into traffic. "We really appreciate it. Um, but I can't stop thinking about what you just told us about Charlie. You don't have any idea why he might have been arrested?"

"Nope." Lionel shrugged. "Surprised the heck outta me. Rumors are already flying back at the shop, though."

"What kind of rumors?" Bess asked.

Lionel shrugged again. "Oh, I dunno. I try not to

listen to that stuff—Charlie's a buddy of mine. I'm sure the truth'll come out soon enough." Just then the cell phone on the dashboard rang. "Excuse me," Lionel said, reaching for it.

He spent the rest of the drive talking to whoever was on the other end about transmissions and clutches. Bess probably understood most of it, but I spaced out after about two seconds and started thinking about Charlie again. No matter how hard I tried, I couldn't figure out what he could have done to get himself arrested. He was one of the most law-abiding people I'd ever known—in all the times I'd ridden with him, he'd never failed to bring the tow truck to a complete halt at a stop sign or follow the posted speed limit.

I still hadn't figured it out by the time we reached our destination. As he turned into the parking lot, Lionel finally hung up the phone.

"Here we are, ladies," he said, pulling up to the big, rawboned metal building that housed Carr's Garage. "You can hop out here and wait in the office if you like. Someone will let you know when your car's ready."

"Thanks," I said. Bess and I hopped out of the cab and watched as Lionel towed my car in through the big, open garage doorway.

"Should we start asking around about Charlie?" Bess asked.

"Why don't you ask around out here?" I suggested, gesturing toward the main part of the garage, a large, open area populated by at least half a dozen men in oil-stained jumpsuits. Several of them were already swarming around my car. If there's one person even better than me at getting information out of men, it's Bess. All she has to do is smile at them, and they'll tell her anything they know. "I'll go see if anyone's in the office."

Bess nodded and headed for the garage area, while I turned the other way and hurried toward the green-painted doorway leading into the small front office. Inside, sitting behind the oversized metal desk, was one of the usual receptionists, a pleasant-faced middle-aged woman named Ruby Carroll.

"Nancy Drew!" she cried as soon as she saw me enter. "Oh, my goodness. Did you hear about our Charlie?"

I nodded. "What's the story, Ruby? What's he accused of?"

"Your guess is as good as mine, Nancy." Ruby shook her head sorrowfully, making the frosted tips of her poufy hairdo bounce. "I can't imagine poor sweet Charlie doing anything wrong—especially not anything wrong enough to get arrested for."

I couldn't argue with the sentiment. "I know," I said. "It's hard to believe. What does Mr. Carr say?"

"He's been out since before it happened," Ruby

reported. "I can't even imagine what he'll say when he hears." She lowered her voice and glanced around carefully. "You know how he gets about this law-and-order stuff."

I grimaced at the thought. Mr. Carr, the owner of the garage and a confirmed bachelor, was a straitlaced ex-military man who had strict standards for himself as well as the people around him. His nephew Jeffrey was a rookie member of the River Heights Police Department, and Mr. Carr liked to tell everyone who would listen that the day Jeffrey had graduated from the police academy was one of the proudest of his life. I couldn't imagine what he would say about having one of his longtime employees arrested right there at his garage.

"Don't worry," I told Ruby. "I'm sure it's all just some kind of mistake." Despite my own words, though, I couldn't help worrying a little myself. Chief McGinnis and his officers might not always be right on top of everything that goes on in River Heights, but I couldn't imagine them making a false arrest of one of the city's most upstanding citizens.

After taking care of the paperwork for my car, I wandered back out into the main part of the shop. One of the mechanics was tightening the lug bolts on one of my tires as Bess watched. When she saw me, she hurried over.

"Find out anything?" she asked.

I shook my head. "You?"

"Nothing too credible," she replied. "Lionel wasn't kidding when he said the rumors were flying. The guys are speculating that poor Charlie's involved in everything from drug dealing to running an international smuggling ring." She shrugged. "Basically, no one knows anything for real."

"Oh, well," I said. "At least it looks like the guys are almost finished with my car. So George won't be able to complain too much about . . . Hey, wait a minute. Where's George? Isn't she back yet?"

"No. And she should be here by now." Bess looked slightly worried. "I wonder what's keeping her."

I shrugged. "Maybe she had to wait for the bus from the pool to here," I said, much less concerned about George's whereabouts than I was about Charlie. "Or maybe practice ran late. Anyway, I'm sure they'll be here soon." Reaching into my pocket, I pulled out my cell phone. "While we're waiting, I think I'll call Ned. He might've heard something about this arrest."

My boyfriend, Ned Nickerson, works part-time for his father, the publisher of the *River Heights Bugle*. He often heard about breaking news as it was happening when he was at the news desk, and I knew he was putting in a full day there today.

When I hit the power button on my phone, nothing happened. I tried again, but the phone didn't let out so much as a chirp in response.

"Great," I said. "It's dead. Do you have yours?"

Bess shook her head. "Sorry. Left it at home." Unlike George, Bess didn't consider herself naked without a phone. "Maybe you could use the phone in the office."

"Good idea." I hurried back into the office, with Bess on my heels. Ruby had disappeared, but I figured she wouldn't mind my making a local call on her phone.

Ned picked up on the second ring. *"Bugle,"* he barked into the phone. "News desk. How can I help you?"

"Ned? Hey, it's me."

"Nancy!" Ned's voice, usually mellow and calm, sounded a bit agitated. "Hey, did you hear what happened?"

"You mean about Charlie?"

"Charlie?" Ned sounded confused. "No, no—I'm talking about the snake."

"Snake?" Clearly we were talking at cross-purposes. "What snake?"

"The fer-de-lance from the River Heights Zoo," Ned replied urgently. "It just disappeared from its display within the past hour or so. Nobody knows where it is."

"Fer-de-lance?" That actually distracted me from my worries about Charlie, at least momentarily. "Really? Those are pretty venomous, aren't they?"

"Very," Ned replied grimly. "Apparently they can be aggressive, too. They're putting out a general alert for people to keep a lookout for it. I can read you the description if you want."

"Maybe later, thanks." Ned's story was fairly interesting news—it's not every day there's a dangerous snake on the loose in River Heights—but I figured it probably wouldn't be long before they found the runaway reptile safely curled up somewhere in the zoo. (I could hope, right?)

My attention was already returning to Charlie's arrest. Ned hadn't heard about that yet, but he promised to look into it for me.

"If you find out anything, call me back on George's cell," I told him, figuring she would be here before he had a chance to get back to me. "Mine's dead."

I hung up the phone. "What was that about a snake?" Bess asked curiously.

As we wandered back out to the main garage, I filled her in on what Ned had told me. "I hope they find that snake before anyone gets bitten. Guess it must've staged a jailbreak."

"Or maybe Charlie snake-napped it, and that's

why they arrested him," Bess said with a grin.

I rolled my eyes. "Very funny," I said, checking my watch. "Okay, so where's George? It really shouldn't take her this long to get back here. Maybe we should . . ."

My voice trailed off as I saw George burst in through the main entrance, her face red and her short, dark hair standing up wildly in all directions. She looked as if she'd just run the whole way from the pool to the garage, though she was still clutching her bus transfer ticket.

"There she is," Bess said, nonchalantly.

"Nancy!" George panted as she rushed over to us. "I tried to call you a million times, but your phone isn't working!"

"I know," I said. "The battery's dead, I guess. Where's Scott?"

"Why can't you keep that stupid thing charged?" George exclaimed, sounding exasperated. "It's really not difficult. You plug the little charger into the socket, then plug the phone into the charger. Do you need me to demonstrate?"

Ignoring her sarcasm, I glanced around for any sign of her younger brother. "Where's Scott?" I asked again. "I think my car's almost done, so if you're ready to go, we can—"

"That's what I was trying to call and tell you," George interrupted impatiently. "Scott never showed up for swim practice!"

"What?" Bess said. "What do you mean, he never showed up? What happened to him?"

"No idea. His coach wasn't exactly thrilled," George said. "He said it's the second time this week he's ditched."

"But I thought your dad dropped him off at the pool during his lunch break," I said.

George shrugged. "He did. But it's not like he held his hand and walked him into the locker room. Scott must have ducked out as soon as Dad drove away."

"But why?" I asked. "I thought he loved swimming."

"He does," Bess agreed. "It's totally his thing these days. He's pretty much the star of the team."

George nodded, scuffing at the cement floor of the garage with the toe of her sneaker. "That's part of the problem," she said. "They've got that big meet coming up tomorrow night, so his coach wasn't too inclined to be understanding about it."

"It's not like Scott to ditch swim practice," Bess said worriedly. "I wonder if he's in some kind of trouble."

"More importantly, what are we supposed to do now?" George said with a frown. "Do I go home and wait for him to show up, or call Mom or Dad, or what?"

I shook my head uncertainly. Scott's behavior was a real mystery. I'd known the kid all my life, and it wasn't like him to act out this way. Was he just being a precocious preteen, or was something else going on, as Bess feared?

Just then the door between the office and the shop flew open with a bang, making us all jump. I glanced over, half hoping to see Scott, though I realized immediately how unlikely that was.

Instead of George's slim, dark-haired brother, I spotted the tall, broad-shouldered, bushy-mustached figure of the garage owner striding in our direction.

"That's Mr. Carr," I said, taking a step toward him as my mind skittered from Scott's odd disappearance back to Charlie's arrest.

The garage owner spotted me at about the same time. "Nancy Drew," he said. "Hello."

I could tell right away that he was upset. Normally, whenever he sees me he chuckles and calls me his "favorite customer"—presumably because I need his services so often. But today he barely flashed me a half-hearted smile before his face returned to a deep scowl.

"Hi, Mr. Carr," I greeted him politely. "We just heard about Charlie, and we're so worried. Can you tell us why he was arrested?"

"That's exactly why I'm here." The man's face and voice were somber, and his mustache was quivering slightly.

Meanwhile, the garage employees had noticed their boss's arrival. Most of them were wiping their hands on rags and hurrying toward us, all of them looking either curious or concerned.

"Charlie got arrested?" George muttered to me, momentarily distracted from her own worries. "What's going on?"

Bess leaned toward her cousin and started whispering rapidly in her ear. But I wasn't paying attention to them. I didn't want to miss whatever Mr. Carr might say next.

As the employees gathered around, Mr. Carr took a deep breath. "All right, people," he said. "I'm sure you're all wondering what's going on with Charlie."

There were nods and murmurs of assent all around. Lionel, Ruby, and the rest of their coworkers were all staring at their boss intently.

I realized my heart was beating fast. Taking a few deep breaths, I reminded myself that this was Charlie Adams we were talking about. Whatever the reason for his arrest, I was sure it had to be some kind of mistake or misunderstanding.

"I just got back from the station house, where I spoke with my nephew Jeffrey," Mr. Carr went on, his scowl deepening. "At first I was certain there must be some mistake when I was told that Charlie had been accused of stealing a poisonous snake from the zoo . . ."

I gasped and glanced over at my friends. George looked more confused than ever, but Bess's blue eyes were wide and startled as she stared back at me.

". . . but while I was there, the call came in over the police band," Mr. Carr continued grimly. "The missing snake was just discovered in Charlie's apartment."

3

Accusations and Alibis

The news of Charlie's arrest was nothing compared to this.

"What?" I cried as a murmur of surprise went through the small crowd around me. "Mr. Carr, are you sure about this?"

"I'm afraid so, Nancy." Mr. Carr pulled at his mustache, looking more upset than ever. "And here I'd just given Charlie a raise and everything. Who could have predicted this? He's been such an upstanding employee—and person—up until now."

"Oh, dear," Ruby murmured, putting both hands to her face. "Oh, dear. Oh, dear."

"A snake?" One of the mechanics, an older man with weathered dark skin, raised his hand, looking confused. "Did I hear you right, boss? Charlie stole a snake? What on earth for?"

Despite the tense atmosphere, there was a small wave of nervous laughter at the man's question. I glanced at Mr. Carr, waiting for the answer.

He barely seemed to have heard. "He had me fooled, that one. Seemed so clean . . ."

I was starting to worry. It didn't seem to me like anyone had proven anything yet. "Okay, let's not freak out, everyone," I spoke up. "This whole situation sounds pretty weird, so we shouldn't jump to conclusions."

Several of the employees glanced at me in surprise, as if wondering why I was sticking my nose in where it didn't belong. But the older man who'd spoken before nodded in agreement.

"Miss Drew's right," he said firmly. "Our Charlie, lifting a snake? Why would someone like him do something like that? It just makes no sense."

Lionel cleared his throat and stepped forward. "Uh, that's not exactly true, Bill," he said, his voice trembling slightly. "See, Charlie is, well . . ." His voice trailed off and he shrugged shyly as all eyes turned to him.

"What is it, Lionel?" Mr. Carr demanded sharply. "If you know something, speak up, son!"

"Charlie, he—he lives near me, right?" Lionel said

uncertainly. "So a few times, he asked me to . . . well, to come by when he was out of town and . . . and . . . check on his snakes."

"What?" Ruby exclaimed. "What do you mean, Lionel? He has pet snakes?"

"Tons of 'em," Lionel replied. "Some lizards and stuff too. I guess he's into, you know, reptiles."

My jaw dropped in amazement. In my investigations I'd often marveled at how many people's ordinary public personas hid extraordinary secret lives—stockbrokers who worked at night as exotic dancers, schoolteachers who raced motorcycles in their spare time, housewives who sneaked off to seedy parts of town to buy illicit drugs—but this was different. This was someone I knew . . . or thought I did, anyway.

"So Charlie is an amateur herpetologist?" I asked Lionel.

He shrugged. "Yeah, I guess. He's really into reptiles."

"A herpe-what?" Bill, the older man, demanded. "Are you telling us the truth, Lionel?"

"Of course!" Lionel looked slightly offended. "You can go peek in his windows if you don't believe me. His whole living room is full of tanks."

"No wonder the cops suspected Charlie when that snake disappeared," Bess murmured as the employees started talking excitedly about this new development. "I guess they knew about his reptile collection."

Mr. Carr stomped off in the direction of the office, looking more upset than ever. "But how?" I said. "It seems like almost nobody knew about it. Not us, or Ned, or most of these guys . . ." I waved a hand at the garage employees, who were all clustered around Lionel by now. "So how would the police know?"

Bess merely shrugged in response. Meanwhile, George had stepped away from the group and was dialing her cell phone, looking worried.

With a flash of guilt, I remembered Scott. I was terribly concerned about the whole Charlie situation, of course. But Charlie was an adult, and I figured he could take care of himself for the moment. Our first priority had to be making sure that Scott was safe.

Poking Bess in the shoulder to alert her, I stepped toward George just in time to see her frown into the phone. "Well, thanks for making me worry!" she said into it. "Not to mention making Nancy drive all over town and ruin her tire . . ."

I breathed out a sigh of relief. Obviously, it had to be Scott on the other end of the line.

"Is he at home?" I whispered.

George rolled her eyes and nodded. "Look, don't run off anywhere else, okay?" she said into the phone.

"I've wasted enough of my time on you. Gotta go." She punched the button sharply to hang up, then blew out a sigh. "Ungrateful little monster," she muttered.

Bess smiled sympathetically. "So he's okay?"

"Yeah." George tucked the phone back in her pocket. "I guess. He got all surly when I started questioning him about it, though. I'll leave the interrogation to Mom and Dad—they're the ones who signed on for this whole child-rearing thing."

I grinned. "Sounds like a plan." My smile faded quickly as I glanced around the garage. "Okay, so that's one mystery solved—sort of, anyway. Now back to this Charlie thing: Do any of us really think he would steal a deadly snake from the zoo, reptile collector or not?"

Bess shook her head, and George shrugged. "Probably not," she said.

There was no "probably" about it for me. Maybe I didn't know Charlie quite as well as I'd thought, but I knew him well enough to be certain that he wasn't a thief.

"Okay," I said briskly. "Then let's get my car, head down to the police station, and find out what's going on."

Luckily my axles and everything else had turned out to be fine, so once I was fitted out with two new tires and the spare was back in its place in the trunk, I was ready to roll. As Lionel pulled my car outside, I glanced around the garage one last time. Mr. Carr had disappeared, and I couldn't help worrying about what he was thinking. Would he give Charlie the benefit of the doubt, or had he already made up his mind?

I shrugged off the question. Maybe I couldn't control what his boss was thinking, but I could try my hardest to prove Charlie's innocence.

"Come on," I said to my friends. "Let's hit the road."

"I hope you don't mean that literally," George mumbled as she and Bess followed me outside.

Despite my friends' fears, we managed to make it the ten or twelve blocks to the police station without any further blowouts or other vehicular incidents. When we went inside, neither Chief McGinnis nor the usual receptionist, Tonya Ward, were anywhere to be seen, though several officers were bustling around behind the chest-high reception desk that separated the rest of the station from the waiting area.

One of the officers, a tall blond detective named Ellen Johansen, spotted me and hurried over with a smile. "Hi there, Nancy," she said. "What can we do for you? Solved any of our cases for us today?"

"Not yet," I joked back, returning her smile. "I

heard my friend Charlie Adams was arrested for that, uh, snake-napping. Is that the correct technical term?"

The detective laughed. "Don't ask me—this one's a first for us!" she said. "And yes, Charlie is here. The missing item—er, snake—was recovered from his domicile. I'm afraid it's not looking good for him so far, Nancy."

I winced. "Can I see him?"

Detective Johansen shrugged. "Don't see why not, if he agrees to it. Hold on, I'll check."

Moments later a clerk was ushering us to one of the holding cells in a back room. Charlie was the only person there. He was sitting slumped over on the hard bench inside, looking confused and dejected. But his face lit up when he saw me, and he jumped to his feet and rushed to the front of the boxy cell.

"Nancy!" he cried, sounding both relieved and embarrassed as the clerk left the room. "They told me you were here. What are you doing here? Never mind—I don't even know what *I'm* doing here; why should I know what *you're* doing here?"

He was talking so fast that all his words jumbled together. I smiled sympathetically at him. "Of course I came when I heard what happened," I told him. "Are you okay? Did you call a lawyer?"

"A lawyer?" He looked alarmed. "Why would I

need a lawyer? I'm innocent! You have to believe me—I don't know how that snake got into my apartment!"

I held up my hands. "I know, I know," I said, though I was secretly relieved to hear him proclaim his innocence. "It's okay, Charlie. I believe you."

"You do?" He smiled shyly, looking slightly awed. "Really, you do?"

"Of course! So do Bess and George. Right, guys?"

Bess nodded vigorously, while George shrugged and muttered, "Sure." She still seemed a bit distracted, and I guessed she was brooding about her brother.

"Okay, then," I said. "Let's figure out how to get the police to believe it too." I wasn't quite sure how I was going to do that, but that had never stopped me before. "What can you tell me about this snake, Charlie?"

He shook his head. "I told you—nothing," he said. "All I know is I'm at work as usual, and the next thing I know the cops are busting in and arresting me." His eyes widened. "I've never been arrested before in my life! Never even *seen* someone get arrested . . . well, except on TV, of course . . . though I don't much care for those cop shows, never really did. . . ."

"Wait a minute." I could tell he was starting to drift, and I wanted to get him back on track. "Did you say you were working when all this happened?"

33

Charlie nodded. "At the garage, from eight a.m., as usual."

"Well, there you go," Bess said. "That's your alibi. Why didn't you tell the police that?"

"I did." Charlie picked at a spot of peeling paint on the cell bars, looking worried. "But see, I wasn't actually *at* the shop when it happened. That's the problem."

"What do you mean?" I asked.

"Right after I get back from lunch, a call comes in for a tow," he explained, grasping the bars with both hands and gazing out at me earnestly. "Unfamiliar name and number—lady says she's from out of state. She's stranded out on Highway Twelve, somewhere out by the old quarry." He waved a hand in the general direction of the flatlands to the south of town.

"Oh." My mind processed that information quickly. "That's about a half-hour drive, right? The police must realize that you still wouldn't have been gone long enough to get over to the zoo, steal the snake, take it to your apartment, and so forth."

"Yeah, except I couldn't find the lady who called," Charlie went on, his brow crinkling with worry. "Car wasn't where she said, so I drove around looking—figured if she was from far away, she might have got the spot wrong when she called, you know?

34

Must have spent forty minutes looking for her before I gave up."

"Uh-huh." I exchanged an anxious glance with my friends. That sounded just like Charlie—he always went above and beyond the call of duty. Of course, that probably wouldn't mean much to the police. At least, not as much as the fact that Charlie seemed to have been out of contact with everyone during the same time period when someone was sneaking that snake out of the zoo. "Uh, did you call in to the garage during that time or anything?"

"Tried to, once or twice," he replied with a shrug. "No answer, though."

I bit my lip. This wasn't looking good for Charlie.

"Do you think you can help me, Nancy?" he asked, gazing at me with a mixture of fear and bashfulness. "Please?"

4

At the Zoo

Okay, so what if he's guilty?" George asked from the backseat.

I glanced at her in the rearview with a frown. "Let's assume, for now, he's not guilty."

"But how do we know for sure?" George tapped her fingers nervously on the back of my seat. "I mean, you're the one who's always saying that you have to consider everyone a possible suspect until proven otherwise, blah blah blah."

"But this is Charlie Adams we're talking about!" Bess protested, twisting around to stare at her cousin. "He wouldn't hurt a fly!"

"Flies aren't the issue here," George retorted. "And nobody's accusing him of hurting anything. But is it so impossible to imagine that he maybe got a little too tempted by a really cool snake he wanted to add to his collection?"

I could tell she was just playing devil's advocate, but my grip tightened slightly on the steering wheel as I realized that a lot of people would probably think the same thing—especially given Charlie's notable and rather odd lack of an alibi. After hearing about the mysterious tow call to the middle of nowhere, I'd spent a few minutes asking him questions about his interest in snakes and the collection at his home.

"Let's not get ahead of ourselves here," I cautioned. "Yeah, I'm still convinced that Charlie is innocent. But we'll see what we find when we get to the zoo, okay?"

Bess pointed. "We're here."

Sure enough, we had just rounded a bend in the North River Road and come within sight of the zoo. Within minutes the three of us were walking beneath the elaborately scrolled iron gates.

The River Heights Zoo sits on several dozen acres atop the picturesque bluffs overlooking the river on the north side of town. It's no match for a big-city zoo, of course, but despite its small size and limited collection, its well-tended animals in their simulated enclosures and its attractive manicured grounds are a source of city pride. The zoo is a destination for school field trips all year round.

"You can get us in for free, right?" George asked me as we approached the ticket window. "Because—"

"I know, I know. You're broke." I grinned and reached for my member ID card. "And yeah, I can get us in." My father, a local attorney, did all the zoo's legal work. Because of that, we had free family passes for life.

Inside, we headed straight for the reptile house. Situated on a private path and half-hidden behind Monkey Island, the reptile house is usually serene and sleepy. At the moment, however, there was a big commotion just outside the glass double doors—at least a dozen zoo workers were calling to one another and rushing around, while several visitors watched curiously from the path nearby.

"Uh-oh," Bess joked, sounding slightly nervous. "I hope nothing else escaped."

I shook my head. "I don't think so." I pointed to a burly man in a blue and yellow zookeeper's uniform. He was carrying a large plastic animal carrier draped in a towel. "I have a hunch the original escapee is just being returned now. Come on, let's see if we can get a closer look."

We hurried forward. When we were still a dozen yards from the action, a young zookeeper charged forward to stop us. "Excuse me—you'll have to stay back!" he told us in a nervous, high-pitched voice.

The young man was so skinny that his blue and yellow uniform fitted him about the same way it would a wire hanger. He wore old-fashioned black eyeglasses that appeared to be in constant danger of sliding right off the end of his long, narrow nose, and his prominent Adam's apple bobbed up and down with every word he spoke.

"Excuse us," I told him politely. "We don't want to get in the way, but we were hoping to talk to those keepers over there about the fer-de-lance."

"I'm sorry, miss," he said politely, his Adam's apple leaping around like a jack-in-the-box. "We need to keep everyone back for now."

Bess stepped forward, flashing the young man her most charming dimpled smile. "Oh, but we're such reptile fans!" she cooed. Peering at the name tag on his uniform, she tilted her head at him. "Couldn't you help us out, Richard—pretty please? We promise we won't get in the way. . . ." Her eyelashes fluttered slightly as she gazed at him imploringly.

Behind her I saw George rolling her eyes at her cousin's antics—but it seemed to work on the nerdy young keeper.

"Well . . . I suppose it wouldn't hurt to let you guys get a little closer," he said slowly, staring at Bess as if she were a fascinating rare specimen from the collection inside. "But don't call me Richard, okay? Only my mom calls me that. You can call me Bones."

Bess let out a giggle. "Okay—Bones," she said, in a tone that could have convinced a Supreme Court justice that Bess had never heard a more delightful nickname in her entire life. "And I'm Bess. This is my friend Nancy, and that's my cousin George over there."

"Hi," Bones said, waving a hand vaguely toward George and me, though his gaze remained on Bess. "Come on this way, and I'll see what I can do, Bess."

"Nice work," I whispered to Bess as we followed him around the edge of the crowd that was gathering to watch the action.

"I have no idea what you're talking about," she murmured back. "I was just making conversation."

George let out a snort, and I stifled a laugh. Bess has a real talent for connecting with people—especially people of the male persuasion. Her pretty face, nice figure, and sunny blond hair help, of course. But the main element that makes it work is her sweet, sincere personality. The world is lucky that she chooses to use her skills for good instead of evil. I'm lucky too—her cute dimpled smile and infectious giggle have helped me out on more cases than I can count.

Bones led us into the reptile house and over to the section known as Snake Street. Gesturing for us to follow him and keep quiet, he ushered us between a tropical rattlesnake and a bushmaster and through a door marked EMPLOYEES ONLY. Beyond the door we found ourselves in a broad, brightly lit hallway running along the back of the display cases where the reptiles lived. A feed cart containing crickets, mice, and various other unsavory items was pushed against the wall near the door, while hooks here and there held nets and ropes and other items that I guessed were used to wrangle the reptiles as necessary.

The other keepers were pouring into the area through a different doorway halfway down the hallway. The burly man we'd seen outside carefully set the covered cage in the middle of the hall. Then he stepped back as another keeper—an attractive, deeply-tanned blond woman in her mid twenties—moved forward. By squinting, I could just make out that her name tag read Edith Fuentes. She seemed to be the person in charge at the moment, since everyone was staring at her expectantly as if waiting for her to tell them what to do. She shot a slightly confused glance in our direction, but Bones gave her a thumbs-up and a grin, and she shrugged and turned away again.

"Okay, guys." Her voice was calm yet commanding as she spoke to the other keepers. "Stand back, please—except for you, Mike. You man the exhibit door while I transfer Isis back inside her home sweet home."

"Isis?" I whispered to Bones.

"That's the snake's name."

I nodded and returned my attention to Edith Fuentes. As the burly male keeper swung open the exhibit's back door, Edith bent down, swept aside the protective towel, and unfastened the top of the plastic carrier. Her movements swift and certain, she reached inside and came up holding a four-foot-long gray-and-brown-patterned snake in both hands.

"Easy, girl," she murmured, her words floating toward us through the slightly tense silence in the hall. "That's it, sweetie. Easy . . ."

With one swift, practiced movement, she swung the snake through the enclosure door and released it. She jumped back, Mike swung the door shut and latched it, and the operation was over.

The other keepers smiled, and a few cheered. "Nice work, Edith," several called out.

Edith smiled. "Thanks, all," she said. "Now let's get back to work."

As the crowd dispersed, I took a step forward. "Where are you going?" Bones said, sounding nervous. "Um, you're not really supposed to be back here."

"I just want to talk to some of the other keepers," I said.

Edith Fuentes, Mike, and an older woman with

curly gray hair were huddled around the back door of Isis's enclosure door peering inside. They all gazed at me in confusion as I approached.

"Who are you?" Edith asked. "How did you get back here?"

"My name is Nancy Drew," I said. "I don't mean to bother you, but I was hoping I could talk to you about that snake's disappearance."

"Nancy Drew," the older woman murmured. "Your name sounds so familiar, dear. Do we know each other?"

I suspected she recognized my name from the newspaper, which often did a little write-up on me after I helped solve some local crime or other—but I didn't say anything about that. When people know I'm a detective, it usually makes them more cautious about what they say, whether they're actually guilty of anything or not.

"You've probably heard of my father, Carson Drew," I told the older woman, whose name tag identified her as Sue Martin. "He's an attorney who's handled some high-profile cases over the past few years." Returning my attention to Edith, I smiled. "You really looked like you knew what you were doing with that snake just now. You didn't even seem nervous."

Edith nodded, lifting one hand to smooth back her

hair. "Thanks. I guess that comes from experience. Put it this way—it's not the first time I've handled a fer-de-lance that didn't particularly want to be handled."

She glanced at the other keepers, who chuckled. Wondering if I was missing the joke, I shrugged. "What do you mean?"

"That particular kind of snake is known to be rather ill-tempered and aggressive," Sue told me. "They'll attack with little provocation, and they're quite venomous as well. Not a snake for a novice handler."

"Oh. So someone actually wanted to steal something like that?" I glanced at Isis, who was calmly curled in her enclosure.

"Yeah, go figure. Happened around one," Mike said. "There was a special feeding demo going on over at Monkey Island, so this place was pretty much deserted." He sighed and shrugged. "I feel responsible, really," he added. "Edith and Sue and most of the others were on their lunch break, and I was the senior keeper here at the time. Should've noticed what was going on."

"Don't beat yourself up about it, Mike," Edith told him. "It could have happened to any of us. Obviously the person who did it had planned it all out very carefully."

"Really?" I said curiously. "Are you sure it couldn't

have been done on a whim? Kids pulling a prank, maybe?"

"Not a chance." Edith shook her head firmly. "Only someone with lots of experience could have pulled this off without getting themselves an arm full of venom. I heard the police already have someone in custody who fits the bill." She nodded and smiled slightly, looking satisfied.

I was dismayed. Obviously she was referring to Charlie, even if she didn't seem to know his name. "But I still don't understand—why would anyone want to steal a snake like that?"

"You'd be surprised," Edith said matter-of-factly. "Plenty of reptile fans would love to add a fer-de-lance to their collections for the bragging rights."

"Bragging rights?"

"Sure. Just the idea of having such a danger ous venomous snake would make the whole thing worthwhile to a certain kind of person."

"Interesting," I said. "So has there ever been a snake-napping here at the zoo before?"

The three keepers exchanged glances. "Not that I remember," Sue answered for all of them. "And I've worked here almost thirty years. But there's a first time for everything, it seems!" She chuckled.

I noticed that my friends had wandered closer while I was talking to the keepers. Bones was still with them, standing right next to Bess. He appeared to be listening intently to my conversation with the other keepers, his Adam's apple still for once. In fact, the intensity of his stare was a little unnerving—sort of like being watched by the cold, unblinking eyes of a deadly snake.

Shaking off that thought, I returned my attention to the other keepers—and the snake enclosure nearby. "So how would someone break in here, anyway?" I asked, noting the solid-looking lock holding the door shut. "Seems like it would be a real challenge."

Edith shrugged again and checked her watch. She appeared to be losing interest in the whole conversation. "It wouldn't really be that hard."

"Edith!" someone called from a doorway a few yards down. "Phone call for you in the office."

"Excuse me." Edith shot me a polite smile, then hurried off.

I watched her disappear through the doorway, feeling slightly frustrated. So far this trip to the zoo wasn't helping me figure out how to clear Charlie's name. In fact, each new detail seemed to support the theory that only he could have swiped the snake.

Sort of, anyway. I, for one, still didn't believe that he was capable of the crime. He just wasn't that kind of person. Besides, I was having trouble imagining anyone—let alone mild-mannered Charlie—having the guts to sneak through this brightly lit, wide-open hallway, and then sneak back down it again smuggling the deadly snake, monkey feeding time or not. Why had Edith commented that it would be an easy thing to do?

Mike and Sue were still standing there watching Isis, and I figured they might be able to shed some light on Edith's last remark. But before I could formulate my question, we all heard a tinny ringing sound from somewhere nearby.

"Oops." George fished in her pocket for her cell. Punching a button, she put it to her ear. "Hello?" She listened for a moment, then her eyes widened. "What do you mean, is Scott with us? He's supposed to be there with you—I just talked to him a little while ago!"

"Uh-oh," Bess murmured as George said a few more words and hung up.

"What is it, George?" I asked worriedly.

"Get this," George said grimly. "Mom just got home, and Scott's nowhere to be found."

5

Search Party

"Okay, let's go," I told George and Bess with a sigh. "We know where Scott likes to hang out—maybe we can find him before your parents freak too much over this."

I wasn't too worried about Scott's safety—with the way he'd been acting lately, I suspected he'd probably taken off just to annoy George and their parents—but still, he was only twelve, and I knew that none of us would rest completely easy until we located him. Besides, I figured I had as much information as I was likely to get at the zoo for now. After thanking Bones for helping us, we hurried out of the reptile house and through the zoo to the parking lot.

"Okay, where to first?" I asked as I punched the

start button on the dashboard to turn on the car's hybrid engine. "Video arcade?"

"Good call." George fastened her seat belt, then slumped back against the seat. "I can't believe that little twerp pulled this. And after I told him to stay put . . ."

"That's probably exactly why he did it," Bess pointed out with a slight smile.

George scowled, not looking amused. As I pulled out of the parking lot and cruised down North River Road in the direction of the city, I decided it might be a good time for a change of subject.

"So what did you guys think of that scene back at the zoo?" I asked.

"Kind of weird," Bess said. "Nobody seemed to have any trouble at all believing someone would steal a snake like that."

"Yeah," I said slowly. "They made it sound like there are all sorts of people out there just itching to get their hands on a fer-de-lance. So that makes me wonder . . ."

"How did they decide to search Charlie's house in particular?" Bess finished for me, clearly on the same wavelength.

"Bingo." Now that the question had entered my mind, it seemed glaringly obvious. "That keeper said the snake disappeared around one, and Charlie was already in custody by the time we called the garage around three this afternoon. How did the police track the missing snake to his place so quickly?"

"Good question." George thought. "Maybe someone tipped them off? A neighbor or a zoo visitor or someone?"

"Could be." I clutched the steering wheel and stared blankly at the road ahead as I turned over the possibilities in my mind. "I guess there's just one way to find out." I glanced over at George. "Can I borrow your phone for a sec?"

George looked alarmed. "While you're driving?"

I rolled my eyes. "Come on," I wheedled. "I'll be careful, I promise. I need to call Chief McGinnis."

George snorted. "Yeah, right," she said, dialing. "Drive and talk on a cell? I don't think so."

"Couldn't we use an earpiece?" I asked. "You've got one, right?"

"Okay, okay," George said, pulling her earpiece out of her pocket and plugging it into the phone. "Here."

She put the earpiece in my ear as the phone started to ring. I got the receptionist, who put me through to the chief right away.

"Nancy Drew," he said when he came on the line. I couldn't help noticing he didn't sound overly thrilled to hear from me. "What can I do for you?"

"I don't know if you heard," I said, "but I was there earlier talking to Charlie Adams. Is he still in custody?"

There was a long pause. "He is," the chief said at last. "Not that it's any of your business, as far as I can tell."

I chose to let the last part pass without comment. "I was just wondering—how did you know to check his place for that missing snake?" I asked. "You guys got there really fast—you must've had a tip or something, right?"

This time the pause was so long that I momentarily feared I'd lost the signal. Finally, though, the chief spoke again. "Look, I'm very busy, Nancy," he said. "I really don't have time to shoot the breeze with you right now."

I winced, recognizing the tone of his voice—when he sounded like that, it meant he was fed up with my meddling and wasn't going to answer any of my questions. I knew I might as well give up right then, but I couldn't resist one last comment.

"Okay, I get the message," I said. "But listen, I was just thinking—maybe you should check the reptile house for fingerprints? You know, see if anyone else was messing around near the enclosure. . . ."

"Thanks for the advice, Nancy," the chief said, sounding outright peevish this time. "As a matter of fact, a couple of my men just left to do exactly that. Not that *that's* any of your business either."

"Sorry, Chief," I said meekly. "It was just a thought."

I heard a snort, then the click that meant he'd hung up. Punching the end button on George's phone, I took a deep breath to fight back a wave of annoyance. Why did the chief always have to be so unhelpful?

"Here you go," I said, tossing George's phone back to her. "Thanks. Not that I found out anything useful."

"Never mind," Bess said soothingly. "He'll be singing another tune if you solve this case for him. In the meantime, here we are."

She pointed out the window, and I realized that I was about to drive right past the arcade. Tapping the brakes, I scanned the block for a parking space. The arcade was tucked into a formerly abandoned storefront between Olde River Jewelers and an insurance office. It was getting close to five o'clock, and the sidewalk was crowded with people walking home from work or running errands before the stores closed. Luckily, a parking spot had just opened in front of the jewelry store, and there were still a few minutes on the meter. I slid into the spot and turned off the car.

"Come on, let's hurry up and check inside," I said,

impatient to find Scott and get back to the snake case. Charlie wasn't going to spend even one night in jail if I could help it.

"Okay. By the way, Nancy, if you're planning to make any more phone calls, why don't you do it while we're stopped?" George suggested as we hurried across the busy sidewalk and into the dim, garishly decorated interior of the arcade.

Ignoring her advice, I scanned the crowd of teenage boys and slacker types clustered in front of the blinking, ringing, buzzing machines. The air conditioner was pumping at full power, and the air was uncomfortably chilly, but none of the arcade patrons seemed to notice. All of them were completely focused on their games, their eyes riveted and their jaws slack.

As I scanned the place for Scott, my gaze bumped into one person who didn't quite fit in with the crowd. Standing in front of a game called Comet Crusher was a pretty, casually dressed young Asian American woman with a shoulder-length dark ponytail.

"Is that Susie Lin?" Bess asked, spotting the woman at the same moment.

George blinked. "Wow. One of these things is not like the other."

I shared their surprise. Susie was the owner of a local bookstore café, Susie's Read & Feed on River

Street. Smart, sociable, quick-witted, and well read, she was just about the last person I would have expected to find spending a sunny afternoon tucked away in the arcade.

Just then Susie looked up from her game and spotted us. Giving us a quick wave, she returned her attention to the machine just long enough to give a few last spins to the controls. Then she left the game and hurried toward us.

"Hey, it's the Three Hungry Musketeers!" she greeted us jokingly, using the nickname she'd given us a few weeks earlier after we'd showed up at her place for lunch four days in a row. "What are you guys doing here? I didn't know you were gamers."

"We're not," I said. "But it looks like you are. Did you sneak out of the kitchen for a little break?"

Susie laughed. "My assistant manager is on duty at the restaurant this afternoon and early evening," she said. "I don't have to be back until the dinner shift. I like to stop in here sometimes for a few games—kind of relive my college days, when I procrastinated from studying at the student center arcade." She chuckled. "You guys here for a little virtual action too?"

Once again I found myself marveling at the surprising variety of people's private obsessions—first Charlie with his reptiles, and now Susie and video games. Then I remembered why we were there.

"We just stopped in here looking for George's little brother, Scott. Have you seen him around here today?" I asked.

"Oh, I know Scott!" Susie exclaimed. "Great kid. He's got the top scores on Alien Face-off and Road Ragers." She shook her head. "But he hasn't been in today since I've been here."

George blew out a sigh. "Stupid little brat," she muttered. "Guess the search continues. . . ." She glanced at Bess and me. "Come on, guys. We'd better keep moving."

Susie gave her a sympathetic look. "I'll walk you out. I need to head back to the restaurant soon anyway."

The four of us stepped out into the late afternoon sunshine, which felt great after the chilled air in the arcade. The street and sidewalk were still busy, but even so, a shrill shriek of laughter caught our attention right away.

"Ew," George said, wrinkling her nose. "Just when we thought this day couldn't get worse . . ."

She was glaring at the source of the laughter: Deirdre Shannon. Deirdre was standing on the sidewalk just outside the entrance to the jewelry store, talking and laughing with a handsome guy I didn't recognize.

"Looks like Deirdre's been shopping at Olde River Jewelers," Bess commented.

George snorted. "I wonder if she was using Daddy's credit card, or if Boy Toy number nine hundred and sixty-eight was paying today."

I smiled. Deirdre has expensive tastes—and thanks to her successful attorney father and a succession of wealthy boyfriends, she always has access to enough money to support them. That tends to annoy George, perhaps even more than Deirdre's less-than-lovable personality.

"Never mind her," I said. "Let's just get out of here before she—"

"Nancy Drew!" Deirdre's voice rang out as she spotted me. She hurried toward us with a smirk, her handsome companion trailing along behind. "Fancy meeting you here," she said, mocking pleasure. "I thought you'd be down at the city jail visiting your good friend Charlie Adams."

I winced. Clearly the word of Charlie's arrest was already making the rounds—which wasn't that surprising to me, since River Heights wasn't all that big. And if there was one thing Deirdre liked better than shopping for expensive baubles, it was spreading mean-spirited gossip.

"Charlie from the garage?" Susie Lin said, looking confused. "What do you mean?"

The rumor mill at work!

"Didn't you hear?" Deirdre's smirk broadened.

"Charlie stole some poisonous snake from the zoo. Who knows what he planned to do with it! Luckily, the cops caught him before he could endanger anyone."

Her voice was loud enough that three or four passersby paused to listen to the conversation. "Are you talking about Charlie Adams and the snake?" one of them asked. The speaker was a freckled young man I vaguely recognized from volunteer group meetings, though I couldn't recall his name. "I heard he's got all kinds of snakes in his apartment—possibly all of 'em stolen from zoos across the Midwest!"

"Oh, dear." Susie shook her head. "I'm sure there's some mistake. I know Charlie, and he wouldn't even steal a paper clip."

"Tell that to the cops." Deirdre shrugged. "They seem pretty sure he's guilty."

Her companion put an arm around her shoulders. "Don't worry, baby," he said, his voice surprisingly high-pitched considering his football-player build. "I'll protect you from any snakes or snake thieves out there."

Deirdre giggled, but the freckled young man and the other listeners all looked concerned. "This sounds serious," said one of them, a middle-aged woman in a suit. Her eyes were wide with agitation. "If that young man is going around town threatening us and our children with dangerous zoo animals, I hope they throw the book at him!"

"Yeah," chorused the freckled guy and another passerby, a tall, thin, older man.

"Lock him up," Deirdre's boyfriend added enthusiastically.

"Whoa, there." I held up a hand. "Let's not get ahead of ourselves. Charlie is innocent until proven guilty, remember?"

Deirdre shrugged. "Whatever. If you ask me, the guy's always been kind of creepy anyway. I'd be happy to see them lock him up for a while, no matter what the reason."

"Nobody asked you, Deirdre," George snapped. "So why don't you shut your stupid mouth for once?"

Susie put a hand on George's arm. "Easy, George," she murmured. "It's okay. This will all work out fine in the end, I'm sure."

I wished I shared her optimism. I wasn't particularly surprised at Deirdre's reaction—she's hardly the picture of fairness at the best of times—but I was worried by the casual way she'd assumed Charlie's guilt, and even more so by the way most of the others seemed be going along with her assessment without even knowing all the facts. If I didn't clear his name quickly, the gossip mill would soon have Charlie tried, convicted, and sentenced to life. If that happened, people were likely to associate him with this crime, no matter how the whole thing played out.

Sticks and stones may break my bones, but words can never hurt me. The words to the old playground chant tumbled through my mind, and I shuddered slightly as I realized they weren't really true. Words could *cause* real problems for people.

In the meantime, we still had to find Scott. "Why don't we check the pizza place over on Fifth Street," Bess suggested after we said good-bye to Susie and headed back to the car. "Scott loves that place. Maybe he went there to meet a friend or something."

"Worth a try," George muttered. She was looking really upset, though whether that was due to the Deirdre encounter or her worry over Scott was anybody's guess.

I climbed into the driver's seat, still thinking about Charlie. How was I supposed to prove his innocence if the chief wouldn't let me in on what was going on?

"Hey, give me the phone again," I said, holding out my right hand toward George as I steered away from the curb with my left.

"What?" She frowned. "I thought we agreed you'd only use the phone while we're stopped. Who do you need to call now?"

"Ned," I said. "I want to ask him if he's heard anything new about Charlie's case. This will be the last call I make while I'm driving—promise. For today, anyway."

George looked reluctant. Bess leaned forward. "Just let her do it," she advised. "You know she'll keep bugging you until you do, and that will distract her just as much."

"Fine," George said petulantly. "But I'll dial, and you're using the earpiece."

Soon Ned and I were comparing notes as I drove through the increasing afternoon traffic. Ned had heard more about the snake case since the last time I'd spoken with him, but he didn't have any new information that I didn't already know.

"I can try to find out more on this end while you guys track down Scott," he offered. "I'll keep you posted."

"Thanks. You can call us on George's cell."

After I hung up, I stuck to my promise by returning the phone to George. With Ned on the case, I felt free to turn my full attention to the Mystery of the Missing Twelve-Year-Old. Over the next half hour or so we checked the pizza place as planned, then his favorite burger joint, the movie theater, and even the bowling alley. But there was no sign of Scott at any of those places. George called home to make sure he hadn't returned in the meantime, but there was no answer.

"Now what?" Bess wondered. "We've looked everywhere."

"Not everywhere," I pointed out. "If the kid doesn't want to be found, there are plenty of places around town where he could be hiding. At a friend's house, out at the mall, in the woods behind the high school . . ."

"I'm sure Mom has called his friends' houses by now," George said. "And she probably—" She cut herself off as her cell phone rang. Grabbing it out of her lap, she answered it quickly. "Hello? Mom?" she said expectantly. Then her face fell. "Oh, Ned, it's you. Um, Nancy can't talk right now—she's driving."

"Give me that." I made a grab for the phone, swerving ever-so-slightly out of my lane and causing Bess to let out a shriek from the backseat. "Come on!" I said, quickly correcting my steering before turning to glare at her. "This could be important."

"Just give it to her already!" Bess cried. "She'll kill us all!"

That seemed a bit overdramatic to me, but it did the trick. George practically threw the phone across the car at me. "Just be careful, okay?" she exclaimed.

I pressed the cell to my ear. "Ned? What did you find out?"

"Nothing you're going to like," his voice responded through the earpiece, sounding rather grim. "First of all, it seems our friend Charlie Adams recently applied for a permit to import a Xenagama."

"A Xenagama?" I repeated. "What's that?"

"From what I understand, it's a rare type of African lizard," Ned replied. "That's about all I know—I never heard of them before. In any case, his application was turned down less than a week ago."

I gulped. "Okay," I said. "That does seem a little suspicious. Still, it's only circumstantial. Is that all you've got?"

"Not quite." Ned's voice sounded more somber than ever. "One of our reporters just called in from the police station. She said they found Charlie's fingerprints all over the reptile house."

6

At the Zoo, Take Two

I gasped. "Really?"

"Really," Ned replied grimly. "And that's not all. One of our reporters also heard that someone reported seeing the Carr's tow truck near the zoo's back entrance around the time of the crime."

"Someone?" I repeated. "Who?"

"Don't know. She's on her way back to the office, so I can try to find out more when she gets here."

I chewed on my lip as I mulled over this new information. The evidence against Charlie was piling up by the moment. Circumstantial evidence, I reminded myself, trying to remain optimistic.

It wasn't easy.

"Thanks, Ned. Talk to you soon," I said, hanging

up. "This stinks," I muttered as I handed the phone back to George. "The more I investigate, the more I feel like I'm helping to prove that Charlie is guilty."

Bess leaned forward from the backseat. "Hmm. But you have to keep going with the case anyway, right? Even if you think he might be guilty?"

"I still don't think that," I answered quickly. Then I sighed again. "But you're right, Bess. I have to keep going, no matter what happens." I glanced at George. "Can I have the phone back?"

Her eyes widened. "You promised! No more calls while we're driving."

Checking my rearview, I quickly swerved over to the curb and threw the car into park. "Okay. Now I'm not driving."

"You realize you're blocking a fire hydrant, don't you?" George grumbled. But she handed over the phone.

I dialed the police station, half-afraid that the chief might answer himself. But this time I recognized Tonya Ward's brisk, no-nonsense voice on the line.

"River Heights Police. Can I help you?"

"Tonya!" I said with relief. "It's Nancy Drew. Is Charlie Adams still in the holding cell there? I need to ask him something."

"Sure, Nancy," Tonya replied without questioning me further. "Just hold on a second."

I waited. There was a click on the line, and then another.

"Hello?" Charlie's voice came on, sounding tentative. "Uh, Nancy? Is that you?"

"Hi, Charlie," I said. "Listen, I don't have long to talk. I just wanted to ask you one question."

"Ask me anything," he answered immediately.

That made me feel a little better. He certainly didn't sound like a man with something to hide.

"I was just wondering if you've been to the zoo lately," I said.

"Sure. I go there several times a week, usually during lunch—I have a membership." He paused. "You heard about the fingerprints, huh? They just came in and told me about that a little while ago. They still think I took that snake. But I didn't! I swear!"

"I believe you, Charlie," I said. "And don't worry, I—"

"Excuse me, Nancy," Charlie interrupted, sounding apologetic. "Chief McGinnis just came in. I guess I'm not allowed any more phone calls or something, because he's telling me to hang up. Thanks for calling, though."

There was an annoyed-sounding murmur in the background, then the faint sound of Charlie saying, "Sorry, sorry." Then a click, and silence.

"Argh!" I said, staring helplessly at the phone in my

hand. I told my friends what had happened. "Okay, so much for case number one. Back to case number two. Where else should we look for Scott?"

"I don't know." Bess pointed out the window. "But there's someone we should ask!"

A kid Scott's age was walking past where we were parked, carrying a skateboard under one arm. George leaned past me to shout to him out the half-open car window.

"Yo, Kenny!" she called. "Have you seen Scott this afternoon?"

The kid glanced over, obviously recognizing George. "Yeah, saw him a while ago," he said, shifting his skateboard to the other arm. "He was in a bad mood or something. Didn't want to hang out."

"Where did you see him?" I called. "Which way was he going?"

The kid squinted at me, as if trying to figure out who I was. Then he shrugged. "Fifth Street," he said. "He was walking uptown. Maybe he was going to the Pizza Palace, I dunno."

"Thanks." George sighed and sat back down in her own seat as the kid moved on. "So much for that—we already checked the pizza place."

"Not so fast." I put the car back into gear. "Just because he wasn't at Pizza Palace doesn't mean he's not somewhere in that area."

Within twenty minutes, we'd finally found him. He was playing solo basketball on the courts behind the elementary school, and he didn't seem happy to be found.

"What are you guys doing here?" he asked sullenly when he spotted us hurrying toward him. Without waiting for an answer, he dribbled the ball and prepared to shoot.

George grabbed him by the arm, making the ball fly off in the wrong direction. "I was just about to ask you the same thing," she said through gritted teeth. "You can explain on the way home. Get in the car—now."

But by the time we dropped him off at his house, we were no closer to an answer. Scott refused to respond to any of George's belligerent questions, insisting that what he did was none of her business.

I was relieved when it was just the three of us in the car again. We'd already arranged earlier that day to have dinner together that evening, so nobody's families were expecting us home until later. That gave us an hour or so to continue the investigation of the snake theft.

"Okay, that's that," I said as I pulled away from George's house. "Can we get back to Charlie now? I want to go back to the zoo and see what we can find out about these new clues."

"Okay." George checked her watch. "We'd better

hurry, though. I think the zoo closes at seven, and it's almost six now."

I grinned. "Did somebody say hurry? Hold on!"

My friends screamed in terror—but I was only kidding, of course.

Even following all applicable speed limits and traffic laws, we found ourselves walking through the zoo entrance less than fifteen minutes later. We each grabbed a slice of pizza at the snack bar, then ate while walking across the zoo to the reptile house. When we got there, we found Bones sweeping the floor.

He looked startled to see us. "Hey, it's you," he blurted, staring at Bess. "Uh, I mean, you guys. What are you doing here?'"

"We just came by to see what was new with the snake situation," I said, keeping my voice casual and friendly. Bones's Adam's apple was bobbing up and down so rapidly, I was afraid it might escape from his throat at any moment. "We heard the police were here earlier."

"Yeah." Bones swept a discarded soda cup into the little pile of trash he was making near the wastebasket. "I guess. That's what Edith said, anyway."

"Is Edith around?" I asked, figuring she might be easier to talk to than the shy and nervous Bones.

Bones shrugged his bony shoulders. "Nuh-uh," he said, sounding annoyed for a moment. "Cut out early today. That's why I'm stuck sweeping—the others won't do it if she's not around to make them."

I was disappointed, but decided to make the best of what I had. At least Bones seemed willing to talk to us, which was more than I could say for certain police chiefs I could mention.

"It's kind of weird how the police got Isis back so quickly, isn't it?" I commented, wandering over to take a look at the snake, which was lying almost motionless in its cage nearby. "Hey, Bones, do you know how they figured out where she was?"

"Nope," Bones said, sneaking a look at Bess, who was fiddling with the hem of her skirt. "I didn't even hear she was gone until after they found her—my shift didn't start until one today."

"Oh." I decided to try another tack. "Um, do you know Charlie Adams, the guy they're accusing of taking Isis? Big guy, brown hair, loves reptiles . . ."

"You mean the tow truck dude?" Bones tore his gaze away from Bess to glance at me. "Yeah, I know him. He comes here a lot."

"Did you see him hanging around yesterday?" I asked eagerly. "Has he been here more than usual lately?"

Bones took a step backward, looking suspicious. "Why would I notice something like that?" he shot back. "I have a job here, you know. I don't have time to be staring at people while I'm working. Not the customers, or—or anyone else." Lowering his head, he dropped the broom against the wall. "Look, I have to go. See you."

Before I could say a word to stop him, he scurried away. A moment later he'd disappeared through the employees-only door.

"Well, that was interesting," George commented, staring after him. "Is it just me, or was he acting sort of . . . guilty?"

"It's not just you." I rubbed my chin thoughtfully, wondering if I'd just found a suspect to replace Charlie at the top of the list. "He really seemed uncomfortable with my questions."

"Hold on." Bess frowned slightly. "I'm not sure you should jump to any conclusions based on that. I've encountered guys like Bones now and then— they get totally tongue-tied talking to anyone of the female persuasion." She winked. "Especially a trio of attractive babes like the three of us. Didn't you notice the way he was checking us out?"

George rolled her eyes. "If you mean the way he kept staring at you . . ."

"It wasn't just me," Bess countered. "He was ogling you guys, too. Not to mention earlier today, when I saw him staring at that head zookeeper."

"You mean Edith?" I stared at Isis, watching as she lazily flicked her tongue in and out. "Maybe you're right, Bess. But it wouldn't hurt to look into this Bones guy a little more. He certainly had the opportunity, right?"

"Sure. But what's his motive?" Bess asked.

"I don't know right now. But maybe George can uncover something about him on the Internet."

"I'll try," George promised. "But maybe Bess is right, Nance. Are you sure you're not just so desperate to find a different suspect that you're suspecting everyone?"

"Of course not!" I said stubbornly. Then I sighed. "Okay, maybe a little. But no matter what the clues say, I just can't convince myself that Charlie is guilty."

Bess shook her head. "I know," she said softly, wandering over to gaze in at a colorful little tropical snake in a nearby enclosure. "It's crazy. But all the evidence is pointing straight at him. I mean, the snake was found in his house!"

"I know." I thought about that for a moment. "I can't stop wondering who might be framing him."

"Why would someone bother?" George asked, leaning against the wall. "Charlie doesn't seem like the type to have that many enemies."

"True," I agreed. "But there was that mysterious tow truck call. Don't you think it's kind of suspicious that he was called way out of town, then didn't find anyone there?"

"Sure," George said. "*If* there really was a call."

"There's one way to try to find out." I held out a hand.

With a sigh, George pulled out her cell phone. "You're chipping in on my overages this month," she warned, handing it over.

"Are you going to call Charlie again?" Bess asked. "They might not let you talk to him."

"Nope. I'm going to call Carr's and see who took that call." I dialed the phone and put it to my ear. "If it was anyone other than Charlie, that supports his alibi, right?"

"Carr's Garage, Ruby speaking."

"Hi, Ruby," I said. "This is Nancy Drew. I just have a quick question for you."

"Is your car all right?" Ruby asked immediately, sounding concerned. "The truck's in; I can send it right out if you need us."

"No, my car's okay." I ignored my friends' amused looks as they listened. "I was just wondering—who was on the phones today around one or a little before? Was it you?"

"No, I came in late today," Ruby reported. "I think Lionel was covering the tow calls, and we let the machine take the rest." She lowered her voice. "Are you still trying to help poor Charlie?"

"Yes, I am," I said. "Have you guys heard anything new from him?"

"Not from him . . ." Ruby's voice quavered, and she let out a loud gulp. "Oh, Nancy, things aren't looking good for that poor boy. Mr. Carr is freaking out about the arrest—he says he's ready to fire Charlie right now!"

7

Guilty Until Proven Innocent

No!" **I blurted out** in alarm. "Ruby, you've got to talk to him! He can't fire Charlie—we don't even know that he's guilty yet!"

"I keep trying to tell him that," Ruby said sorrowfully. "Hey, here he comes now—maybe he'll listen to you."

I heard a rustle of movement, and a moment later Mr. Carr's voice came on the line. "Yes?" he barked. "Who's this, please?"

"H–hello, Mr. Carr," I stammered, caught off guard. "This is Nancy Drew."

"Ah, my favorite customer." His voice softened slightly, though he still sounded tense. "What can I do for you, Miss Drew? Those new tires working out so far?"

"Yes, fine, thanks." I swallowed hard, trying to figure out how to phrase what I wanted to say next. "Um, Mr. Carr, you've heard about my amateur detective work, right?"

"Of course! I've often told your father he must have raised you up right," Mr. Carr said. "He should be proud of you, helping to uphold law and order in this town."

"Thanks. Well, I heard—I heard you're . . . worried about Charlie. You know, with the arrest and everything . . ."

"Worried doesn't quite cover it."

"Right. I understand that." I took a deep breath. "But see, I think Charlie is innocent. And I'm working as hard as I can to prove that. So I'm hoping that you . . . that you . . ." I hesitated, not wanting to insult him by implying that I thought he was jumping to conclusions—even though that was exactly what I did think. "That you give me a chance to get some answers before you do anything about this," I said finally in a rush. "Before you do anything about, you know, Charlie's job or whatever."

There was a long pause. Just when I started to wonder if we'd been cut off, he finally spoke again. "I hope you realize what you're asking me to do, Miss Drew."

"I think I do. Really."

"I'm sure you know that I take right and wrong and following the law very seriously. That's why I put my life on the line in the service, and it's why I'm so proud of my nephew for doing his duty on the River Heights force now." He sounded stern. "If Charlie was involved in this crime, he's not the same young man I always thought he was. I won't have my good name and my business associated with someone shady. Just wouldn't be appropriate."

"I understand. But like I said, I'm pretty convinced that he's innocent."

"Fine. I'll wait—if you say so, Miss Drew." He sighed. "What a day," he muttered, less to me than to himself. "Here I just gave the boy a raise, and then he has to go and get himself involved something like this. . . ."

I wondered uneasily if he'd heard a word I'd just said about not judging Charlie before all the facts were in. Still, he'd promised to wait before making any drastic moves. And if there was one thing I knew about Mr. Carr, it was that he would stand by his word.

"Okay, then," I said. "I'll be in touch. Oh, but before I hang up, I was wondering if Lionel is around. I was hoping to talk to him—I heard he answered the tow call Charlie got this morning."

"Lionel? He's gone home for the day," Mr. Carr said. "I'll let him know you were asking for him when he comes in tomorrow, though."

"Thanks." After his fiery law-and-order speech, I was afraid to ask for Lionel's home address or phone number. Somehow I wasn't sure Mr. Carr would find giving out his employees' personal information "appropriate."

I hung up and started to tell my friends what the garage owner had said. "We know," George interrupted almost immediately. "We could hear him. He's got a voice like a bullhorn." She reached to take back her phone. "Want me to call Information and see if we can get Lionel's digits?"

"I have another idea." I turned and headed for the reptile house exit door. "We already know he lives near Charlie, and we're only a few blocks from their neighborhood right now. Let's just drive over there and see if we can randomly run into him—so he doesn't suspect."

During the time I'd had my car, I had chatted with Charlie often enough in the cab of his tow truck to know where he lived. Less than half a mile from the zoo, their neighborhood was made up of modest two-story houses that had been built in the 1950s as single-family homes but had since been mostly converted into rental apartments.

My friends seemed a bit dubious about the plan, wondering if we'd be able to find him that way. But as it turned out, we spotted Lionel as soon as we turned onto Charlie's block. He was in the driveway of a house just across the street from Charlie's place, tinkering with the engine of a red car.

"Whoa." Bess let out an appreciative whistle as we approached. "Check it out—looks like Lionel has an old Mustang! Nice."

I glanced at the car. It just looked like an ordinary old car to me, but what do I know? George appeared similarly unimpressed.

Lionel seemed surprised to see us when I pulled up to the curb by the end of the short driveway and waved to him. "Hi," he called, wiping his hands on a rag. "What are you guys doing here? Is there a problem with the tires?"

"No, nothing like—"

"Cool Mustang!" Bess gushed, interrupting me as she jumped out of the backseat and hurried over for a closer look at Lionel's car. "Is it yours? What year?"

"Yep, she's my baby. A sixty-seven—I wanted a sixty-five, but they're pretty pricey for a guy on my salary." He grimaced slightly. "So anyway, when I saw this girl, I knew she was for me." Lionel beamed proudly as Bess ran her hand gently over the vehicle's gleaming hood. "Had her about six months, and she's just about where I want her. I'm just saving up for a few more parts, and then she'll be perfect."

"Really? What parts do you still need?"

With that, the two of them launched into a bunch of

gearhead talk that mostly flew over my head. I waited as patiently as I could through their incomprehensible discussion of rotors and intake manifolds. Lionel was obviously thrilled that one of us was showing an interest, and I figured he'd be more helpful if he was in a good mood.

Finally, though, I'd had enough. It was getting late—the sun was already sinking down toward the horizon, and as far as I knew, poor Charlie was still sitting in the city jail.

"Listen, Lionel," I said, interrupting some question Bess was asking about shifty gears. Or maybe it was gearshifts—who knows. "We didn't just stop by to check out your wheels. I heard you were the one who took the call that Charlie was on when the snake disappeared. I was hoping you could tell me anything you remember about the person who called."

Lionel looked disappointed to have his car talk cut off so abruptly. "Uh, okay," he said dubiously. "But if you're thinking there was something mysterious about the tow call, you're probably wasting your time. Charlie drives like a little old lady—by the time he got all the way out there by the quarry, the lady probably got tired of waiting and called another garage." He shrugged. "Happens. I keep telling Charlie he needs to step up the pace if he doesn't want to lose customers."

"Duly noted," I said. "But what can you tell me

about it? All Charlie mentioned was that the caller was a woman."

"Her name was Sue. She didn't give a last name. Guess I should have asked." He shrugged. "I don't work the phones that often, you know?"

"Sue?" Immediately my mind flashed to the kindly, gray-haired zookeeper we'd met earlier. I recalled somebody—Bones? Mike?—mentioning that she'd been out to lunch when Isis had disappeared. My heart thumped, and I wondered if I was about to add another name to my suspect list.

George must have been thinking the same thing. "So how old did this lady sound?" she asked eagerly.

Lionel pondered that for a moment. "Young," he said at last. "Maybe twenty? I dunno. But definitely young, I think."

So much for that theory—Sue definitely didn't sound very girly. I exchanged a disappointed glance with George. "Okay, and did she say anything else?" I asked Lionel.

"Just that she blew a tire and didn't have a spare." He grinned. "Hey, just like you, remember?"

"Not quite," Bess corrected. "Nancy had a spare, she just happened to be using it to drive on at the time."

Lionel laughed. "Zing!" he exclaimed, giving Bess a high five. He glanced at me. "So is that all you wanted to know?"

I didn't answer for a moment. My mind was turning over all the facts I had so far, trying to fit them together in a way that made sense—and that *didn't* involve Charlie stealing that snake. So far the phone call was the only thing that seemed to offer an alternate path to investigate. Who was the mysterious Sue? And why had she disappeared before the tow truck arrived? Was it really just that Charlie had driven too slowly, or was something else going on?

Thank goodness Lionel picked up that call, and not Charlie himself. Otherwise it would just be his own word that the lady with the blown tire existed at all. I'd still believe the call happened, of course—but would anybody else?

As I glanced across the street toward Charlie's house, I had another idea. "Lionel, you said you sometimes feed Charlie's reptiles for him, right? So you must have a key to his place."

"Uh-huh," Lionel said, brushing a spot of lint off his car's hood. Then he glanced at me, his eyes narrowing and his face taking on a slightly scandalized expression. "Wait a minute—you're not asking me to let you in there, are you?"

I shot him my most appealing smile. "I'm sure Charlie wouldn't mind," I wheedled.

I guess I'm not as good at wheedling as Bess is, because Lionel shook his head firmly. "Sorry, Nancy," he said. "You seem like a nice, honest girl and all, so no offense, okay? But I just wouldn't feel right letting you in there without his specific permission. Especially with the police crime-scene tape still up and everything."

Glancing across the street, I saw that he was right—bright yellow tape marked off the side entrance to the house where Charlie's apartment was located, flapping slightly in the evening breeze. "Well . . ." I kicked Bess in the ankle as a subtle hint that I could use some help.

Bess looked up from studying the car. "Oh," she blurted out. "Um, are you sure you can't help us out, Lionel? It wouldn't be big deal, really—Charlie and Nancy have been friends for ages."

It wasn't particularly flattering to notice that he looked a lot more tempted by her request than by mine, but I was used to it. "I don't think so," he told her with a shy smile. "But hey—we could go for a ride in my 'Stang if you want." Shooting George and me a glance, he added with far less enthusiasm, "Uh, your friends could probably fit in the backseat if they want to come too."

I shot Bess a meaningful glance and an almost imperceptible nod. She frowned slightly at me, then turned back to face Lionel. "Um . . . sure," she said. "Sounds fun, I guess."

"Yeah," I piped in with an innocent smile. "But maybe George and I will stay here and wait for you. That backseat doesn't look too comfortable."

Lionel didn't try to change our minds. "Cool. Come on," he told Bess eagerly. "Key's already in it. Wait until you see how she handles on the curves."

A moment later Lionel, Bess, and the red car roared off down the street in a cloud of exhaust, disappearing around the corner at the end of the block. I rubbed my hands together and smiled.

"What are you looking so happy about?" George demanded. "And why'd you let her go off with him? It's getting late, and we're nowhere near solving this thing, as far as I can tell."

"Right," I agreed. "That's why I needed to get rid of Lionel for a few minutes. See, when I asked him about getting into Charlie's place, I noticed that he glanced over toward that door." I nodded toward a battered-looking screen door leading into the first-floor apartment at the top of the driveway. "If you'll notice, there appears to be a key-shaped wooden key rack right inside there."

"You mean . . . ," George began, looking slightly alarmed.

I smiled, finishing for her. "We're going in whether he agrees or not!"

8

Sssssss . . .

It takes a lot to shock George, but my pronouncement seemed to do the trick. Her jaw dropped.

"What?" she sputtered. "Are you nuts? That's, like, breaking and entering."

"Not really." I shrugged. "I'm one hundred percent positive that Charlie would give us permission to go in if he could."

George couldn't really argue with that. "Okay," she said after a moment. "I guess you're right. But I'd hate to see you try to explain that to Lionel if he catches you—or to Chief McGinnis."

"That's why you're going to stand guard outside while I go in." I was already hurrying up the driveway toward the screen door, which turned out to be not only unlocked, but slightly ajar. Finding the right key was easy—using my amazing sleuthing powers, I quickly deduced that it had to be the one on the lizard-shaped keychain.

None of the other neighbors were in sight at the moment—everyone was probably inside eating dinner—so we hurried across the street without bothering to hide what we were doing. We stopped in the driveway near the cordoned-off door.

"Okay, stay out here," I told George. "We don't know how long Lionel will be gone, so give a loud whistle or something if you see him heading back." I lifted the key, preparing to fit it into the lock. But as soon as my hand touched the door, it swung open.

"Nice," George commented. "The cops must've forgotten to lock up when they left with the snake. I'm sure Charlie will appreciate that if he gets robbed tonight."

I smiled. "We'll lock up when we're done. Now wish me luck!"

With that, I pushed the door open the rest of the way and stepped inside. I found myself in a mudroom containing a washer and dryer and a small collection of umbrellas and boots. It was dim inside, and I almost tripped over a stray sneaker, but I avoided the temptation to turn on the overhead light. I didn't want to call attention to myself, just in case any of those neighbors looked up from their dinners at the wrong moment. Squinting and willing my eyes to adjust quickly to the lack of light, I moved forward.

There were two doors leading off the far end of the narrow mudroom, and I chose the one aiming toward the front of the house. When I pushed through it, I found myself in a surprisingly spacious living room. The plate-glass windows overlooking the street were covered by pale fabric shades, but enough of the fading daylight seeped through to cast a dim glow over everything. The air felt warm and close, with no hint of air conditioning. There was a worn sofa in front of the window and a couple of wooden chairs pushed up against the walls, but aside from that, the room was entirely taken up with enormous glass tanks set on low tables.

I stepped cautiously toward the closest one and peered inside. A fat green lizard stared back at me, its tongue flicking in and out of its mouth without making a sound. As my eyes adjusted further to the dim light, I glanced around and saw that I was surrounded by reptiles.

I walked around the room, glancing into one tank after another. Although I'm no expert, I recognized a few of the snakes—a corn snake, a couple of garter snakes, even what I was pretty sure was a small coral snake. But there were lots more that I couldn't identify. A bright green snake, and one with orange spots. Three pretty little jewel–like frogs. A large lizard that I thought might be an iguana. Almost every one of the two dozen tanks appeared to be occupied, though there were two or three empty ones stacked in the corner.

"Quite a collection, Charlie," I murmured, impressed. It was clear just from looking around this room that Charlie approached his hobby in the same careful, thoughtful, conscientious way he did his job. Every tank was spacious and scrupulously clean, furnished with real tree branches and rocks to create comfortable habitats for his pets.

Although I'm not the kind of girl who screams every time she sees a snake or a mouse, I couldn't help feeling a shiver being in the presence of so many reptiles—especially when I noticed the distinctive diamondback pattern of a large rattlesnake curled up in one of the tanks. When I stubbed my toe on a table leg, making it scrape across the wooden floor, I jumped about three feet in the air. And when a floorboard creaked upstairs, I almost tripped over the tank of colorful frogs.

Forcing a laugh, I put one hand on my racing heart. "Okay, Drew, chill out," I muttered. The minutes were ticking away, and as I'd told George, I didn't know how much time I would have to look around. I couldn't let myself start freaking out at every little noise.

I headed through an archway on one side of the room, which led through a windowless little area that Charlie seemed to be using as a library—the two solid walls were lined with tall, mismatched wooden shelves crammed with books. At the far end of the library, another archway led into a small but tidy kitchen, which was dominated by a round wooden dining table. Sitting in the middle of that table was another tank—this one much smaller than the ones in the other room, and not nearly as clean. Thick smudges marred the cloudy glass, and there was a small crack near the top. The water in the flat dish inside smelled rank, and the only other furnishings in the tank were a few small rocks.

"Weird," I muttered. "Not exactly a snakey Taj Mahal—"

I cut myself off as I heard a soft thump. It sounded as if it had come from the next room, and for a moment my heart raced, my mind filled with the image of Lionel coming in and catching me. But after a moment of listening, the sound didn't repeat itself.

Duh. Of course someone's moving in the next room, I reminded myself. I'm sure those reptiles move around in their tanks all the time. I'm just freaking myself out over a lizard jumping down from its tree branch for a snack or something. . . .

My gaze wandered back to the empty tank on the

kitchen table. Judging by the matte bootprints criss-crossing the otherwise shiny linoleum, I guessed that this was where the police had found the fer-de-lance. I wrinkled my nose, wondering why Charlie would stick his prized acquisition in the small, grimy tank when there were several larger, cleaner tanks in the next room that appeared to be empty.

"Quarantine?" I murmured uncertainly. It seemed as good a theory as any, though it still seemed odd that he wouldn't at least clean up the holding tank a little better.

That's if he was the one who did it, I reminded myself, a little uneasy as I realized I was starting to think as if Charlie had stolen the snake. Maybe this dirty little tank could be a real clue to a frame-up.

Still pondering that, I took a look around the rest of the kitchen. There were two doors opening off of it. The first opened into a small hallway leading to a bedroom and bath. The other opened back into the mudroom through which I'd entered.

I walked back into the library. A beam of red-dish sunlight angled into the room through the kitchen window, allowing me enough light to read the names of the books on the shelves. While there were a couple of sections of paperback novels and a few other books, most of the titles I could see were related to reptiles and amphibians. There were books on caring for various types and species, scientific tomes about them, books of photos, and more.

I crouched down to get a better look at some of the titles on the bottom shelf. At that moment there was another soft thud from the next room, but this time I forced myself not to jump like a silly schoolgirl. Instead I ran my fingers lightly across the spines of the books on the shelf, ignoring the sound.

As my finger stopped on a book about pythons, I heard another, louder thud directly behind me, followed by another noise, also much closer than the next room. The latter was a quieter but much more unsettling sound, sort of like a dry pinecone clattering along the ground. I turned my head—and froze in terror.

Just two or three feet behind me, its head raised to strike, was an enormous rattlesnake!

9

Looking for Motives

For a long, breathless moment, I couldn't move a muscle. I crouched there in the dim room staring at the snake. It stared back at me with its catlike eyes. Its tongue flickered in and out, and it let out another ominous rattle with its tail. I gulped, my throat going dry.

Now what?

I was trapped between the snake and the bookshelves. If I tried to dart around it, it was likely to react to the sudden movement and strike. Could I sneak past it more slowly? Experimentally, I put one of my hands on the floor, preparing to rise.

The snake rattled again, its head weaving slightly from side to side. I froze.

Okay, bad idea, I thought, feeling myself on the verge of panic. I remembered reading somewhere that rattlesnakes were fairly bold and therefore unlikely to back down once coiled to strike. Giving in to what seemed inevitable, I started calculating whether George would be able to hear me if I screamed for help, or if I'd have to crawl or stagger to the door to let her know to dial for an ambulance. But I kept getting distracted by wondering fearfully exactly how much it would really hurt to have those long, deadly, venom-filled fangs sink into my arm or leg. . . .

"Nancy! Hold still!"

The snake and I both jumped. Glancing toward the kitchen end of the library, I saw Lionel standing in the doorway, with Bess and George right behind him. Their faces were pale with fear as they took in the scene.

"Don't move a muscle," Lionel whispered as the snake let out another warning rattle and regathered itself.

I wasn't sure if I could have moved just then anyway, but I didn't bother to mention that. Lionel disappeared for a moment and then reappeared in the opposite doorway. He was holding a very long, very sturdy-looking set of tongs. Before my frightened brain could wrap itself around this new development, he took several swift steps forward.

Before I or the rattlesnake quite realized what was happening, Lionel grabbed the snake with the tongs a few inches behind its large, flat head. As soon as it felt itself trapped, the snake reacted violently, flinging itself around trying to escape. Its long body and narrow tail whipped back and forth, slapping me hard against the shins as I leaped to a standing position.

"Get out!" Lionel yelped. "Quick—to the kitchen. Out of the way."

He didn't have to tell me twice. I darted past him, sustaining one or two more tail-whippings on my way. A second later I was collapsing into Bess's arms.

"Are you okay?" she cried, hugging me tightly. "Nancy, did it bite you?"

"No," I said weakly. "No, you guys got here just in time."

I turned to watch as Lionel dragged the still-struggling snake across the floor with the tongs. I held my breath, not even wanting to think about what might happen if the tongs slipped or he lost his grip on the handles.

A few long moments later, he had disappeared into the reptile room. I'm guessing none of us took a breath until he reappeared, sans snake and tongs, in the archway. "There," he said, his voice shaky. "It's back in its tank."

"Whew!" George blew out an explosion of relief. "Wow, Nancy. How did you—how did that—just *how?*"

"I don't know." Now that the moment of danger

had passed, my wits were returning. "I'm pretty sure that snake was in one of the tanks when I came in. At least, I'm pretty sure I saw a rattlesnake out there—I remember noticing the tail. So if that was the same snake, how did it get loose just now?"

Lionel shrugged. "Who knows?" he said. "Come on, we should get out of here."

I stared around thoughtfully, hardly hearing him. "You know, I thought I heard some noises while I was looking around," I mused. "Guess I should've paid more attention to them."

Lionel looked alarmed. "Noises?" he said, glancing around quickly. "What kind of noises?"

"Sort of thumping, I guess. Like I said, I wasn't really paying that much attention—I figured it was just the reptiles moving around out there." I nodded toward the front room.

"You're probably right," Lionel said immediately. Then he paused. "Um, but then again . . ."

"What?" I demanded, sensing that he was holding something back.

"Well, I guess you deserve to know." Lionel took a deep breath. "See, Charlie sometimes likes to let some of his little friends roam free in his house. Get some extra exercise, I guess."

"You mean when he's not home?" I blinked in surprise. "Are you sure?"

Lionel shook his head. "I tried to tell him it didn't seem like such a hot idea to me," he said. "Made sure he locked 'em all up anytime I was supposed to come by. But other times, well . . ."

"Are you serious?" George said. "Charlie let poisonous snakes slither around this place on the loose? That's crazy!"

"He used to joke about it, say they were better than a German shepherd," Lionel said weakly.

I was astounded by what he was telling us. Charlie was nothing if not a careful person, from everything I had ever known of him. Then again, I was starting to wonder if I'd ever really known the real Charlie Adams at all.

"Look, you guys should go outside," Lionel said urgently. "I'll take a quick look around, make sure nobody else is on the loose. No other snakes, I mean. I'll be out in a minute."

Still deep in thought, I allowed myself to be shooed out through the kitchen and mudroom, along with my friends. Soon the three of us were standing in the driveway outside the back door while Lionel ducked back inside.

"Are you sure you're okay, Nancy?" Bess asked, still looking concerned. "You seem a little shaken up."

"I am. But not because of the rattlesnake," I told her.

"You're not mad at me, are you?" George asked anxiously. "I was keeping watch, I really was. But then my mom called on my cell phone, and by the time I spotted the car coming back, he'd already seen me standing here, and—"

"Never mind," Bess said soothingly. "Considering how things worked out, it's just as well."

"True." I gulped, flashing back to that eerie rattle. Forcing my mind off that topic, I glanced at Bess. "So how was your ride, anyway?"

"No problem. It's a very nice car," Bess said diplomatically.

I smiled, guessing that Lionel hadn't turned out to be her dream date. "Well, thanks for going," I said. "I only wish I'd managed to find out something useful because of it."

"So, nothing?" George asked.

Kicking at a stone in the driveway, I shrugged. "Not much." I filled them in on everything I'd seen, including that grimy tank in the kitchen. "Seems kind of odd he'd just plunk his new snake in there, doesn't it?"

"Sounds kind of odd to steal a deadly snake from the zoo in the first place," George countered.

I sighed, knowing she was right. A few smudges on a tank weren't going to convince the police that Charlie was innocent if everything else pointed to his guilt. "Okay, guess it's time for a new plan," I began. "It's getting late and the zoo is closed, but maybe tomorrow—"

I cut myself off as Lionel reappeared. "All clear," he said. He frowned. "And by the way, what's up with the breaking and entering, anyway? I told you I didn't want you going in there without permission."

"Sorry," I said, trying to sound contrite. I handed him the key to Charlie's apartment. "I was just trying to help Charlie." Before he could continue his scolding, I changed the subject. "So, Lionel, you said you help Charlie with his reptiles sometimes. How long has he been collecting them? Where did he get most of them? How did he learn about taking care of them? Does he have any favorite types or anything?"

"Whoa." Lionel held up both hands and smiled wryly. "You're asking the wrong dude. Yeah, I sometimes poked my head in to make sure everyone was still alive if Charlie went away for the weekend or something. But he really didn't talk to me much about the details of his little zoo. He mostly discussed that stuff with his buddies from the River Heights Reptile Society." He wrinkled his nose. "Well, at least until recently."

"Oh?" I'd never heard of the group, though that was no surprise. "What happened recently?"

Lionel glanced around quickly, as if afraid someone might be eavesdropping. "Well, I don't know all the details," he said. "But I guess Charlie was having some kind of fight with one of the other members."

"A fight?" Once again, this didn't sound like Charlie. That was becoming a familiar refrain. "What do you mean?"

"Yeah, I heard it was because the other person got a spitting cobra for their collection, and Charlie was all kinds of jealous." His eyes widened. "Hey! Do you think that's why Charlie might've decided to grab that snake today? Kind of even the score?"

The thought had occurred to me as soon as Lionel had mentioned the society spat. "Let's not jump to conclusions," I said hastily, feeling a twinge of guilt. This case was looking worse for Charlie all the time.

Could I have misjudged him all this time? I worried silently. And how would I be able to face him if I was the one who proved he did it?

Ten minutes later Bess, George, and I were back in my car heading for home. I was pretty quiet as I drove, thinking over what had just happened. I guess my friends must have thought it was due to my close encounter with the rattler and taken some pity on me, because for once they weren't complaining about my driving at all.

Finally George broke the silence. "So," she said. "It's not looking too good for Charlie, is it?"

"Not really," I admitted. "But the more I think about it, the less the whole case makes sense."

Bess leaned forward, looking surprised. "Really? But now we have a possible motive," she pointed out. "I hate to say it, because I've always liked Charlie, but the whole jealousy thing kind of makes sense in a weird way."

"I know," I said slowly. "I was just thinking about that. Charlie never seemed like a competitive, envious type of guy. But then again . . ."

"He never seemed like the type of guy who had ninety gabillion creepy crawlies in his living room, either," George finished.

I smiled slightly. "True." My smile faded. "But . . ." I hesitated.

"What?" George demanded. "What are you thinking? I believe I detect a strong whiff of a patented Nancy Drew hunch."

That made me smile for real. My friends are always teasing me about my hunches, pretending they're some weird supernatural ability I have. But I suspect they're aware of the truth: My hunches usually come from solid information that my conscious mind hasn't quite managed to process yet. For that reason, I usually trust them.

"Maybe a little one," I said. "But it's not about Charlie, exactly. It's about Lionel."

"Lionel?" Bess asked.

I nodded, easing to a halt at a red light. "I sort of wonder if he's been trying to cover for his buddy Charlie," I said. "Something about the stuff he's been telling us—even the way he didn't want to let us into Charlie's house—it just seems a little off, you know? But I can't quite put my finger on why."

"Want to stop off at my place and check him out?" George offered. "It won't take long to Google us up some info on Mr. Lionel Hart."

I checked the clock on my dashboard as I accelerated through the traffic light, which had just turned green. "Sure it's not too late? It's almost nine."

George shrugged. "Trust me. After the way my little bro acted today, I'm sure my folks are still up yelling at him."

That was a bit of an exaggeration. When we arrived at George's house, her parents were watching TV in the den, while Scott was nowhere in sight. After saying hello, the three of us headed straight upstairs to George's room. Bess and I flopped onto the bed to wait while George headed for the cluttered desk that held a large portion of her collection of electronic and computer equipment.

She fired up her laptop and was soon searching

the Internet for any useful information about Lionel. Before long she'd discovered his middle name (James), his date and place of birth, and more.

"There's a bunch of stuff about his family on a family tree site I found," George said as she leaned forward, scanning the tiny words on the screen. "Looks like his parents are divorced, both still living, and he has, like, three siblings and a bunch of cousins and stuff. Want me to go into that more?"

"Don't bother," I said. "Try linking him with Charlie—see if you can find out how long they've known each other."

Soon that information, too, was at George's fingertips. "Check this out," she said. "Looks like they went to high school together, right here in River Heights!"

"Really?" I sat up a little straighter. "Interesting. So they're not just coworkers and neighbors. They've known each other a while."

Bess shrugged, examining her fingernails. "So what?"

"So maybe Lionel has even more reason than I thought to try to help him," I mused, thinking out loud. "Could he have made up that mysterious caller named Sue to try to give Charlie an alibi?"

George turned around in her computer chair. "I guess," she said, not sounding convinced. "But then why would he tell us about all the intrigue or whatever at the Reptile Society?"

"Good question," I said. "I'm not sure where that fits in. Can you look up the society, as long as we're at it?"

"Sure." George spun around and went back to work. Seconds later a website flashed onto the screen. Even from halfway across the room, I could read the name "River Heights Reptile Society" at the top of the page.

I stood up and wandered over for a closer look. The home page was clearly an amateur job, with little in the way of graphics. It seemed to consist mostly of a bunch of reptile-related links and a small amount of basic information about the group, including a list of its officers.

As I scanned the officer list, I gasped out loud. "Check it out," I said, pointing to the first name on the list. "The president of the Reptile Society is named Sue!"

10

What's in a Name?

By the next morning I'd almost convinced myself that the name had to be a coincidence. Sue was a common name; there had to be dozens, if not hundreds, of women who shared it in the River Heights area. Still, I figured I'd better look into it just in case.

I stared into the bathroom mirror as I brushed my teeth, almost wishing I'd never involved myself in Charlie's case. But what else could I do? Charlie was a friend, and I was trying to help him. If things turned out badly for him . . . well, I had to do my best to find the truth all the same. What kind of detective would I be if I backed off just because the primary suspect was a friend?

That made me feel a little more righteous, but not much happier. Quickly tying my reddish blond hair back into a ponytail, I left the bathroom without another look in the mirror.

When I arrived at George's place, she and Bess were waiting for me in the Faynes' kitchen. When I walked in, George waved a couple of sheets of paper at me.

"Here you go, Nancy," she said. "I printed out that list of Reptile Society names and addresses."

"Cool. Thanks." I took the papers from her and glanced at the top sheet. "Did you double-check their meeting schedule?"

"Yep. They don't have anything scheduled until next month, so I guess we'll have to track down the lizard lovers one by one." George paused. "Or at least you and Bess will. I just found out I have to drive Scott to his swim practice again, then run some errands—Mom has a catering job tomorrow and I'm on shopping duty. Dad's letting me use his car."

"Bummer. Maybe you can meet up with us later."

"Yeah. Call me if you find anything interesting."

I was still scanning the list. "I think I already did," I said, pointing to a name. "Look—Richard 'Bones' Smith. And here's Michael J. Carucci—wasn't that the other zookeeper's last name?"

"I think so. Guess it's no surprise that reptile keepers would join the local Reptile Society." Bess leaned over my shoulder to look. "Hey, there's Edith, too."

I looked where she was pointing. "Edith Hart Fuentes," I read aloud. "Hart? That's Lionel's last name."

"Wow," George commented. "Do you think they could be related?"

I stared at the name thoughtfully. "It could just be a coincidence. Then again, it would certainly explain how he knew exactly what to do about that loose rattlesnake yesterday."

Just then Scott walked into the kitchen. He was dressed in swim trunks, a T-shirt, and flip-flops, and he'd slung a towel over one shoulder. His face was twisted into a disgruntled scowl.

"Come on," he muttered to his sister. "If I'm late, I'm telling Coach it's your fault."

George rolled her eyes. "Yeah. I'm sure he'll be real sympathetic after the way you ditched yesterday," she said. "Especially with your big meet coming up tonight." She got up and grabbed a set of keys off the counter. "Catch you guys later. Don't forget to call if you find anything."

Once the two of them were gone, Bess and I headed out to my car. "So where does President Sue live?" Bess asked as she opened the passenger side door. "I guess we're going to talk to her first?"

"Guess again," I said with a smile as I slid into the driver's seat. "I figured we should talk to some of the other members first—you know, feel them out about this whole feud story. If it's true, Sue might deny it anyway."

"Oh! Good point. So where should we start?"

I turned on the car. "In the one spot where we can find at least three or four members in one place, of course," I said. "The zoo."

When we arrived, it was still early enough that there were only a few cars in the parking lot. We found a nice, shady spot near the entrance and climbed out of the car.

"This is a weird case, isn't it?" Bess commented as we strolled toward the gates.

"What do you mean?"

She shrugged and tossed her hair over one shoulder. "Usually you're busy trying to prove someone is guilty. This time you're trying to prove someone's *not* guilty."

"That's not true," I argued. "I just want to find out the truth."

She glanced over at me, arching one perfectly groomed eyebrow. "Really?"

I grinned sheepishly. "Okay, so maybe it's a *little* true," I admitted. "I mean, I'm hoping the truth turns out to exonerate Charlie."

"Yeah. But how likely is that?"

I sighed. "Okay, maybe not quite as likely as I'd

hope." I quickly ran over the evidence in my mind. "I mean, Charlie certainly has the interest in snakes, there's no denying that. But I have an interest in chocolate, and that doesn't prove I'm going to go out and rob the candy counter at Mason's Drugstore."

Bess giggled. "Good thing," she joked. "If we were going by that sort of 'proof,' George would be tossed in jail anytime something got stolen from the local electronics store."

We had reached the gates by now, and I paused to flash my membership card at the guard. Then we continued on our way into the zoo, wandering down the by-now-familiar path leading toward the reptile house.

"Anyway," Bess said, picking up the conversation more or less where we'd left off, "it might not be proof, but I think you can safely say that Charlie seems to have had the motive and the means to pull this off."

"Maybe." I brushed away a pesky fly that was buzzing around my head. "But we don't know for sure if there's really anything to Lionel's feud story. And despite Charlie's reptile expertise, I'm not totally convinced it would be that easy for him just to walk in and steal that snake—no matter what was going on at Monkey Island at the same time."

"He has poisonous snakes of his own, obviously."

Bess shuddered visibly, clearly thinking back to the previous day's close encounter. "He must know how to handle them."

"True. But that's not what I meant. It just seems like someone would have spotted him. That fer-de-lance was pretty big—whoever took it must have used something pretty big to carry it out. Don't you think someone would find it suspicious to see anyone but a uniformed keeper carrying around a big box or carrier like that?"

"Maybe he used a backpack or something?" Bess shook her head. "I wish I could still totally believe Charlie was innocent, Nancy. But think about it—they found the thing in his house. What's that saying about how the most obvious solution is usually right?"

"I know, I know." I bit my lip.

We hadn't reached any new conclusions by the time we reached the reptile house. Inside, we found Bones near the Gaboon viper exhibit in the Rain Forest Hall. He looked surprised to see us again.

"Boy, you guys really like reptiles, huh?" he commented.

"Sort of," I said with a smile. "You must be really into them too, right? We heard you're a member of the River Heights Reptile Society."

"Yeah," he said. "Most of us here are." He waved a hand toward the employee door.

I stared at the viper in the cage in front of us. Deciding to leave my questions about Charlie's alleged feud for later, I took advantage of the private moment with Bones to ask him about what Bess and I had just been discussing.

"So it's hard to believe someone actually managed to steal one of these guys," I commented, gesturing toward the snake. "Wouldn't it be pretty hard to break into these enclosures without a key?"

"Yeah," he answered. "I was wondering about that too. That guy who took Isis must've swiped a key. Otherwise it would be practically impossible."

"No, it wouldn't," a new voice added.

Turning, I saw Edith Fuentes striding toward us, a steaming Styrofoam cup of coffee in one hand. "Oh, hello," I greeted her politely. "I was hoping to run into—"

"I heard what you just said, Bones," she said irritably, pretty much ignoring me. "You know, some people around here aren't as careful as they could be." She spun to face me with an apologetic smile. "We always make sure the place is locked up tight before we leave in the evening. But during the day, I'm afraid sometimes we slip up. I imagine that fellow who took Isis must have sneaked into the back hall when we were all busy and just checked the enclosures until he found one that wasn't locked."

"Oh, yeah," Bones said immediately, sounding sheepish. "You're totally right, Edith. I dunno what I was thinking. I guess I was thinking it happened at night or something. Duh!"

She took a sip of her coffee and shot him a glare over the rim. "Well, try thinking a little harder next time."

"Sure thing." He glanced at his watch. "Oops, gotta go. Time to start checking water dishes." With that, he disappeared down the hall.

I elbowed Bess. "Follow him," I whispered as Edith turned away to wipe a smudge on one of the glass cage fronts with a rag from her pocket. "See if you can get him to talk any more."

Bess nodded and hurried off. When Edith turned to face me again, she looked a bit surprised to see me standing there alone. "Well, if you'll excuse me," she began, starting to move off.

"Do you have a moment?" I asked politely. "Because I'd love to ask you a few more questions about this snake-napping case."

"Case? What case?" She shrugged, making her coffee slosh in the cup. "The police already have the criminal in custody. So what's to ask?"

She probably meant that as a rhetorical question, but I answered anyway. "What's to ask is whether they really have the right person," I said. "Charlie Adams is a friend of mine, and I'm just trying to make sure he's not being falsely accused."

"I don't see how there can be any question," Edith replied with a frown. "They found the snake in his kitchen. How much more evidence do you need?"

I decided to try a different approach. "I don't know," I said. "But I was chatting with a coworker of Charlie's yesterday, Lionel Hart." I paused, feigning surprise. "Say, I think I read somewhere that your full name is Edith Hart Fuentes. Any chance you're related?"

She hesitated, taking a long sip of her coffee. "Yes," she said at last, lowering her cup and reaching up to brush back her hair with her free left hand. "Lionel is my little brother. Maybe I should ask him if he thinks—oops!"

As she lowered her left hand, she knocked herself lightly in the right forearm, causing that hand to jerk forward. The coffee cup flew out of her grip—and showered its contents all over my shorts and T-shirt.

"Whoa!" I cried, jumping back—but it was too late. Luckily the coffee wasn't hot enough to burn me, but my clothes were dripping with the brown liquid.

Edith gasped, both hands flying to her mouth. "Sorry!" she cried. "Oh, I'm so clumsy. . . . So sorry, Miss Drew."

"That's okay," I murmured politely, pulling a stray tissue out of my pocket and dabbing at my shirt. "No big deal."

"No, it is," she insisted. "And I really am so, so sorry. Here, why don't you come in the back? You can rinse off in the employees' washroom. In the meantime, I'll send someone over to the gift shop for a clean shirt—on the house, of course."

"No need for that." I waved away the shirt offer. "But I'll take you up on the restroom part."

She showed me back into another section of the same hallway I'd seen the day before. Leading me along it and around a corner, we came out into a large, brightly lit, lablike area where several other zoo employees were bustling around busily. I spotted Mike, the keeper I'd seen the day before, carefully reaching into a tank sitting on the counter. Nearby, the older keeper, Sue, was mixing something in a small bucket. A couple of unfamiliar keepers were present as well, and several reptiles of all shapes and sizes were lounging in tanks and cages on the counters and center island tabletop.

I barely had time to take in the scene—and the keepers' looks of surprise at my coffee-spattered state—before Edith had whisked me through a swinging door on the far side of the room. In the narrow hallway just beyond, she pointed out the restroom.

"Go ahead," she said. "There should be plenty of soap and towels and stuff in there. Take as long as you like."

"Thanks." I let myself into the restroom. It was small, with only three stalls and a couple of sinks, and unoccupied aside from myself.

As the door closed behind me with a soft *whoosh*, I wandered toward the mirror over the sink to check out the damage to my clothes. Although I was annoyed about the accident, I welcomed the moment of privacy to think over what I'd just observed and heard.

Bones is definitely an odd one, I thought as I grabbed a paper towel and bent over to dab at the front of my shorts. He practically turned himself inside out agreeing with Edith when she turned up. What's up with that?

My thoughts turned next to Edith herself. She had been completely dismissive of my investigation. Was that because she had information I didn't about what the police had found—or could it be because she didn't want me poking into it any further? My mind flashed to an image of Lionel, then back to Bones again.

Swoosh. I heard the bathroom door swing open and shut again.

"Hi," I called to whoever had entered, staying bent

over just long enough to wipe up another couple of spots from my shorts. "Sorry, I'll just be a minute, I . . ."

My voice trailed off as I straightened up to face the mirror. There was no one visible behind me. Puzzled, I turned and glanced around the small room. Empty.

Then I heard a weird sort of scratching sound. Shifting my gaze downward, I found that the little room actually wasn't quite empty after all.

With a gulp, I stared at the two-foot-long, black and yellow spotted lizard advancing rapidly toward me, its mouth open and its claws skittering across the tile floor. I wasn't quite sure what it was, but I didn't like the look in its beady little eyes.

"Yikes!" I gasped out, leaping aside just in time to avoid the lizard's attack. The creature turned and kept coming, its blunt tail whipping around, its mouth still gaping open threateningly to reveal a lower jaw full of teeth . . . and its thick, spotted body between me and the door.

11

Setting a Trap

Quickly rejecting the idea of trying to jump over the lizard—who knew how fast the dinosaur-like creature could move, or how high it could jump?—I instead dashed toward the only potential safety I could see, namely one of the stalls. Leaping inside, I immediately jumped atop the toilet rim—there was no seat—and perched there, hoping against hope that the lizard couldn't jump or climb the smooth porcelain bowl.

The creature followed me as far as the open stall doorway. It paused there, as if it was stymied by the sudden disappearance of my feet. The important thing was that it stopped, and its mouth slowly fell shut.

My sneakered foot slipped, almost plunging into the blue-tinted water below. I caught my balance just in time. It wasn't too comfortable crouching there, but I figured it probably beat the alternative.

"Okay, this is getting really old," I muttered, more annoyed than frightened by now, as the lizard moved its head from side to side and took a couple of steps forward.

I stared at it, wondering if I was overreacting. For all I knew, this imposing-looking lizard could be some sort of mascot for the reptile house; perhaps it was some kind of harmless pet that was allowed to roam freely through the halls.

Rrrring! Rrring!

The sudden tinny jangle startled me so much that I almost fell into the toilet again. Reaching into my pocket, I fished out my cell phone and stared at it in surprise.

Rrrring! Rrring!

It rang again in my hand. The sound echoed off the tiled room, startling me anew and almost causing me to drop the phone into the water. I was so surprised that it was actually charged up and functioning—my father or our housekeeper, Hannah Gruen, must have charged it for me—that it took yet another ring before it occurred to me to answer it.

"H-hello?" I stammered out.

"Nancy? Hey, it's me." George's familiar voice poured into my ear. "Listen, you're never going to believe how Scott the Snot was acting on the way to swimming. You'd have thought *he* was the one doing *me* a favor by deigning to be in the same car as me! I mean, seriously. I was about ready to dump him off by the side of the road and let him walk the rest of the—"

"Um, George?" I interrupted. "Listen, I'm kind of in the middle of something. But as long as I have you on the phone, do you have handy access to the Internet right now?"

"Sure. Why?" She sounded a bit disgruntled at being cut off.

"Can you check and see if there's any such thing as a poisonous lizard?" Shooting a glance at the spotted creature, which was by now lying motionless in the stall doorway, I added, "Especially ones about, oh, two feet long or so, with sort of black and yellow spotted skin."

"Uh, okay. If you say so." My friends are pretty accustomed to fielding odd requests from me when I'm in investigation mode, so she didn't ask any further questions. "Hold on."

Pressing the phone to my ear, I waited, keeping a cautious eye on the lizard. There was the faint sound of a clicking keyboard, and then George came back on the line.

"According to the website I found, there are only

two species of venomous lizards in the world," she announced. "And based on the photos I pulled up, it looks like they're both around the size and coloring you mentioned. They're the Gila monster and the Mexican beaded lizard. Both are native to deserty-type parts of North America, and—"

"Okay," I interrupted. "That's really all I needed to know. See, I'm sort of being stalked by one right now." At that moment the lizard in question, which had been lying quite still in a rather nonstalking fashion, decided it was time to start moving around again. It scuttled a few inches closer to the toilet tank and looked up. "Oops. Look, I have to go. I'll call you in a little while—maybe."

"What?" George yelped. "Wait, Nancy, I—"

I hung up and tucked the phone back in my pocket. Now that I knew I actually was in danger, I decided it was time to do something about it. Unlike at Charlie's house, I wasn't really scared this time—just irritated, sort of like the Gila-beaded whatsit itself.

Standing carefully on the edges of the toilet bowl—the lizard had slumped back into motionlessness, but I figured if it did decide to try to come up there after me, I might as well not give it a shot at anything higher than my ankles—I took a deep breath. "HELP!" I shouted at the top of my lungs.

"HELLOOO! IS ANYONE OUT THERE? HELLLLLLP!"

The bathroom door opened within seconds. From my perch, I could see a confused-looking Bones standing there.

"Bones!" I cried. "Look out—lizard on the loose."

He had already spotted the creature. A look of horror crossed his face. "Whoa, how'd Chompers get in here?" he exclaimed. "Don't move, okay? That's a Mexican beaded lizard—very venomous, and sort of cranky. You don't want him to bite you."

"What does he think I'm doing up here?" I muttered to the lizard, rolling my eyes as Bones disappeared from the doorway.

He was gone for what seemed like a very long time, though it was probably only a minute or two. Just when a little voice in my head started whispering, *What if he just locked the door and left you in here with this thing?* the door opened again. This time Bones was wearing heavy gloves and holding a large carrying crate.

"Just hold tight," he told me as he moved cautiously forward.

Within a moment or two it was all over. Chompers was latched inside the crate, and several other people were gathered in the hallway, drawn by the commotion. Bess was among them.

"Nancy, what happened?" she cried, rushing forward as soon as the lizard was safely out of the way.

I climbed wearily down from the toilet tank. "I seem to be a magnet for deadly reptiles these days, that's what," I told her, pulling her aside and quickly outlining what had happened. "Did you happen to notice who came running when they heard me screaming?" I added.

"I'm not sure. I was so worried myself. . . ." Visibly pulling herself together, Bess glanced around. "I know Bones was already here, of course. And I'm pretty sure I saw Mike, and that keeper with the red hair, and a couple of people I didn't recognize."

"What about Edith and Sue?" I asked, recalling that Sue had been in the lab-type area when I'd passed through.

"Oh yeah, Sue, too," Bess said immediately. "I didn't see Edith, though."

Mike was just outside hoisting the carrier with Chompers inside it, while Bones and several others looked on. I hurried toward them.

"Hey, do you guys know where Edith is?" I asked.

Bones shrugged, but Mike nodded helpfully. "She said she was ducking out to the cafeteria for more coffee," he told me. "Hasn't come back yet."

"Thanks." I smiled at him as Bess yanked me away. "What's the matter?" I asked her when we were once again out of earshot.

120

"Things are getting kind of scary," she said. "This is the second time in two days that someone's sicced a deadly reptile on you."

"I noticed," I said dryly. "Once could have been bad luck, but twice? I'm thinking somebody is getting nervous. And it's not Charlie."

Bess's eyes widened. "Good point," she said. "I have to admit, I thought you were grasping at straws before with the whole framing theory. But it's starting to look like you were right. Somebody really doesn't want you to figure out what happened here yesterday."

I smiled at her, glad that she was fully on board. "Bingo. And if they're that worried, you know we're getting too close for comfort."

"So what do you want to do?" Bess still had a worried look in her eyes, but she squared her jaw bravely. "Are you ready to track down the mysterious Sue and see if she knows anything useful? Or should we try leaning on Bones a little more?"

"Nope." I winked at her. "I'm pretty sure I've figured out exactly what went down. All we have to do is set a little trap so I can prove it. . . ."

"You look perfect, Ned!" Bess cried, clapping her hands gleefully.

"Yeah," George put in with a smirk. "Nobody

would ever know you weren't a real sleazebag, dude."

"Thanks." Ned Nickerson rolled his eyes and let out a long-suffering sigh.

Smiling at my boyfriend, I squeezed his shoulder fondly. Then I returned my full attention to my task of tracing one last fake tattoo on his right bicep. The four of us were in Bess's room, putting the finishing touches on Ned's disguise. He was dressed in battered jeans, work boots, and a cheap, dirty T-shirt Bess's mother had been using to wipe bug splatters off her car windshield. His handsome face sported a bushy fake mustache, and his hair was hidden beneath a shaggy, shoulder-length black wig.

"There," I said, stepping back and capping my pen with satisfaction. "Who ever said I wasn't an artist?"

George peered at the tattoo dubiously. "What's that supposed to be—a snowman?" she asked.

Bess smacked her on the arm. "Stop!" she chided. "It's a snake, of course." She smiled at me. "It looks awesome, Nancy. Really."

Ned flexed his bicep, glancing down at the coiled cobra, which I had to admit did look a little like a fat green snowman from a distance. "Hush up, wimmin-folk," he said in a low, growly voice. "There's a *man* talkin' now."

We all burst out laughing. "Perfect," I declared.

"Talking like that and looking like that, even your own family wouldn't recognize you."

"Maybe," Ned said in his normal voice. "I just hope I can pull this off."

"You'll be great," George assured him. "Now hold still and let me attach your wire."

"Where did you get that equipment, anyway?" I perched on the edge of the bed as George busied herself attaching a tiny microphone to the inside of his shirt collar.

She glanced over her shoulder at me and grinned. "If I told you, I'd have to kill you."

Bess rolled her eyes. "Do you even need to ask, Nancy? George has to have every electronic gadget ever invented, remember?"

"And today, aren't you glad about that?" George retorted. "Otherwise this plan would never work. And you said it yourself, Nancy—this could be our last chance to clear Charlie's name."

"But no pressure, right?" Ned put in, sounding a little nervous.

"Don't worry," I told him. "You can do it. Just stick to the plan."

Twenty minutes later I eased my car to a stop in an alley around the corner from our destination. It was about two thirty in the afternoon, and the streets in that part of town were nearly deserted. It was a few blocks to the nearest residential area, and most of the local workers had long since finished their lunch breaks. The alley was completely still and silent, except for a scruffy little dog nosing around in the trash cans at one end.

"Okay, let's do this," I said briskly, glancing over my shoulder into the backseat, where Ned and Bess were sitting. "Ned, you can walk over from here—we definitely don't want anyone to see you getting out of my car." As much as I love my hybrid, it's pretty distinctive-looking, and a lot of people around town know it belongs to me.

In the passenger seat in front, George nodded and patted her laptop, which was balanced on her knees. "We'll be able to hear everything you say," she said. "Just stick to the script and speak up."

"Got it." Ned took a deep breath. "Here goes nothing. Wish me luck." He slipped into his tough-guy voice. "And that's an order, ladies!"

We all obeyed as he climbed out of the car. He walked normally almost to the end of the alley, then broke into an uncharacteristic swagger that perfectly matched his fake persona.

I grinned, watching him. "That's my boy," I murmured.

George glanced over at me. "Are you sure he can

pull this off? I mean, Ned's more the Dudley Do-Right type than the tough-guy type."

"He can do it," I said confidently. "Hurry, turn on the machine." I gestured at her computer.

She flipped open the top, and it flickered to life. "Ready to go."

For a moment all we could hear were the sounds of footsteps and breathing. "Wow," Bess commented. "That microphone works great."

"Yeah, it better," George said. "It cost me more than—"

"Shh!" I said urgently. "I hear voices."

A moment later Ned's voice crackled through the speakers, so loud that we all jumped. "'Scuse me, buddy," he barked out in his tough-guy voice. "I'm lookin' for a dude name of Lionel—Lionel Hart. You know him?"

"I—I'm Lionel," another voice squeaked, sounding decidedly nervous. "Um, do I know you?"

"Dude!" Ned chuckled. "No, you don't know me—yet. But I been hearin' about you."

"What do you mean?" Lionel sounded cautious.

"C'mere, man. This is private."

There was a moment of muffled walking noises, then a sound that had to be a door clicking shut. "Good," I said. "I told him to try to get him off by himself, where he's more likely to speak freely."

Because I was talking, I missed the first part of what Ned said next. But I heard Lionel's response.

"My sister?" he said. "Wait, what did she tell you?"

"Come on." Ned's gruff voice took on a jovial tinge. "You don't have to front with me, man. Your sister told me the whole story. Way to go—you're, like, some kind of genius!"

"I don't know what you're talking about, man!" This time Lionel sounded outright alarmed. "I didn't do anything wrong."

"You don't have to tell me, brother. You did everything right. How'd you come up with such a slick plan, anyway? Your sister think it up? She seems like a smart one, that girl. I mean, I only know her from the Reptile Society meetings, but she seems cool, you know?"

There was a long pause. "Well, as a matter of fact, it was almost all *my* idea," Lionel said. His voice still sounded nervous, but a hint of pride crept in as well. "I mean, I couldn't have done it without Edith, obviously. But she mostly just helped me fine-tune the basic plan, you know?"

I held my breath and exchanged a glance with my friends. Despite my confident words earlier, I hadn't been completely sure that Ned would be able to get Lionel to talk. But he was doing it!

"Cool." Ned chuckled admiringly. "Yo, but why'd you do it? Edith didn't fill me in on that. And hey— you don't have to spill your secrets either if you don't want to, man. I'm just curious, is all."

"It's okay." Lionel sounded downright eager to talk now. "See, I've been working at this stupid place for, like, two years, and I'm making almost the same money as when I started, while goody-two-shoes Charlie keeps getting raises and first dibs at the tow truck calls."

"So you decided to do something about it, huh?" Even through the microphone it sounded like Ned's fake voice was slipping a bit as he shifted into reporter mode. I held my breath. Don't push too hard, Ned, I thought. Don't give yourself away.

Luckily, Lionel was too caught up in his own story to notice that this stranger seemed a little too interested in his life. "Yeah. I thought about it for a while, and I came up with the perfect idea," he bragged. "See, I knew I had no shot at that tow truck gig—and the extra dough that comes along with it—as long as Charlie was here. Mr. Carr, like, worships the dude." There was a slight pause, and I could imagine Lionel rolling his eyes for effect. "So I thought, what's the best way to get him fired? Answer: convince straight-arrow Mr. C that his teacher's pet is actually no good. First I tried starting some rumors about Charlie around the shop—you know, drugs or whatever—but nobody was buying that. So I came up with this. I knew if he got arrested, he'd be out. And since Edith works at the reptile house and Charlie has the snake fetish, the rest was pretty much a no-brainer."

"Cool." I was relieved to hear that Ned's fake voice was back. "Guess smarts run in your family."

"Wait. But why are you here, anyway? Why'd Edith tell you about this?" Suddenly he sounded suspicious, and I held my breath.

"Just gettin' to that, man." Ned's gruff voice still sounded natural and easy, and I couldn't help admiring his acting skills. "See, I happened to mention to your sis that I'm looking for someone to help me out. Take care of some unpleasant business, you could say. Catch my meaning?"

"Not really." Lionel sounded nervous again now.

"These snakes of yours." Ned cleared his throat and lowered his voice slightly, though we could still hear him just fine, thanks to the sensitive microphone. "These deadly snakes . . ."

"Hold on a second!" This time Lionel sounded downright panicky. "I think you have the wrong idea about me. See, I was never going to hurt anybody—I told you, I just wanted to get Charlie fired so I could get myself a little more money to help pay for my car and stuff. No big deal."

"Look, man. You just said you need money, right? And I'm willing to pay—very well." Ned's voice lowered still more to a deep, menacing purr. "All I need you to do is handle the snake part for me. I'll take care of the rest."

"Okay, I think we have enough," I said as, over the microphone, Lionel started protesting again. "Come on, let's go break this up."

George nodded. "Too bad. Sounds like we were just getting to the good part," she quipped.

We climbed out of the car and hurried around the corner, still listening in as Ned continued the charade. George was recording the entire conversation on her computer's hard drive, just in case Lionel tried to deny it later—although I didn't think he would. I suspected that this confrontation with exactly what he'd done—and what kind of person it made him appear to be—just might be knocking some remorse into him.

When we walked into Carr's Garage, several mechanics were working on a minivan in the main part of the shop, and Ruby was visible at the reception desk through the glass-topped office door. I glanced around, trying to figure out exactly where Ned and Lionel might have gone for their private chat. Now that we had what we needed, I didn't want to make him suffer any longer than necessary—Ned seemed to be really relishing his role as a tough guy and was leaning on him pretty hard. I almost felt sorry for Lionel as we listened to him beg Ned to go away and leave him alone.

"Poor guy," Bess said, echoing my thoughts, as Lionel's voice sputtered up through the computer. "He really sounds freaked out."

George snorted. "Yeah, poor guy," she said sarcastically. "Bet he didn't worry about how Charlie's felt sitting in the pokey for the last twenty-four hours."

She had a point. But her comment also reminded me that the sooner we put an end to this charade, the sooner Charlie would be a free man again.

"Is that the employee washroom back there?" I nodded toward a door near the office. "Maybe they're in there."

"Let's check it out," Bess said.

As we headed for the door, I spotted Mr. Carr out of the corner of my eye. He was striding toward the same door. He noticed us standing there and veered toward us.

"Hello, Miss Drew," he said. Nodding at Bess and George politely, he added, "Ladies. What can I do for you today?"

"Hi, Mr. Carr," I said. "As a matter of fact, we were about to come looking for you. There's something I think you should—"

"NO!" Lionel shouted at that moment, so loudly that we could hear his voice faintly from beyond the washroom door as well as over the microphone, which George had turned down a little when we came inside. "Just because I'm willing to mess around a little with goody-goody Charlie doesn't mean I'm willing to kill somebody!"

Mr. Carr heard it too. "What?" the garage owner roared, hurrying past the three of us and throwing open the washroom door. "What's going on in here?"

A startled Lionel looked out at us. His mouth opened and closed several times as he stared at his boss, but no sound came out. Ned casually looked over his shoulder and turned toward Mr. Carr.

"What do you mean, you messed around with Charlie?" Mr. Carr demanded. "Speak up, boy—I want an answer right now!"

12

One Last Mystery

By the time Bess, George, and I settled into the pool bleachers for Scott's swim meet a little before six o'clock that evening, it was all over. We'd all been busy since Lionel's confession a few hours earlier, and we'd ridden over to the pool together with George's entire family in their minivan, so this was our first chance to talk over the case privately.

"So what's the latest, Nancy?" Bess said as she settled onto the echoing metal bleacher seat. "Are Lionel and his sister all settled into their jail cells?"

I chuckled. "I'm sure they're out on bail by now," I said. "But they're still in serious trouble. There are plenty of people ready to testify against them—Charlie is so sweet that he was ready to not press charges against either of them, but I don't think the zoo is going to be so forgiving. Not to mention Mr. Carr."

Mr. Carr had fired Lionel on the spot, even before calling the police to turn him in. Then he'd insisted on driving down to the station to pick up Charlie himself—and apologize.

"Yeah, Mr. Carr was pretty fired up this afternoon. You're lucky he didn't drag Ned off to jail along with Lionel," George joked.

I grinned. The garage owner had been pretty suspicious of Ned at first. It was only after I'd vouched for him—and ripped off his fake mustache—that he believed Ned was with us.

"I know," I said. "Still, it was kind of lucky that Mr. Carr came along just then. Saved us the work of proving what we'd found out."

"I still can't believe Lionel went to all that trouble just to get a better job." Bess shook her head in amazement. "I mean, I know he loves that car of his and wants more money to finish fixing it up. I can't blame him for that. But to frame a nice guy like Charlie over it? That's low."

"He had to go through a lot of effort to do it too," I pointed out. "This wasn't something he just did on impulse; he had to work it out pretty carefully. First he had to pick a time when Charlie was on tow truck duty and Edith was working at the reptile house. Then Edith had to make sure none of the other keepers were around so she could sneak that snake out without arousing suspicion."

George nodded. "I guess once she was away from the reptile house she was okay," she commented. "If any of the keepers from other parts of the zoo saw her carrying an animal cage, they wouldn't think twice about it. But her own people might wonder or ask her what she was doing."

"Right," I said. "Plus I imagine she had some kind of backup story just in case someone did see and put two and two together later when they heard about the missing fer-de-lance. I doubt someone like Edith would have left anything to chance."

"So then Edith took the snake over to Charlie's?" Bess asked. "I guess Lionel must have given her the key, or made sure the door was unlocked."

"And don't forget that tow call," George put in. "They had to time that just right to ensure that Charlie would be off without an alibi at just the right time."

"Uh-huh," I agreed. "And then as soon as Charlie got back to work, Edith placed another call—this time to the police station as an anonymous tip. Actually, I think she claimed to be a concerned neighbor or something. That's how they found the snake so quickly." I shrugged. "I guess despite everything, she was worried about Isis's safety—didn't want to leave her unattended for too long. At least that's what she said down at the station house."

Bess sighed and brushed her blond hair away from her face. "It all just seems so complicated."

George leaned back and rested her elbows on the empty bleacher seat behind her. The meet wouldn't start for another ten minutes, and the spectators were still arriving.

"I sort of wonder if that might have been part of the thrill for Lionel, actually," Bess said thoughtfully. "All that underhanded, intricate plotting . . . it must have been sort of like an elaborate game or something, sort of like those video games Scott loves so much. I mean, let's face it, Lionel doesn't seem like the most mature guy on the planet."

"I hadn't thought of that." I glanced at her, impressed by her insight. "Although I think he also just didn't like Charlie very much, dating all the way back to their high school days. At least that's the impression I got from Lionel after he confessed. By the way, in case you didn't already figure it out, he totally made up that whole feud story. He was just trying to throw us off, I guess."

Meanwhile, Bess was staring thoughtfully down toward the cool blue expanse of the pool. "Okay. But the part I still don't get is why his sister went along with it all," she said. "Yeah, Lionel is kind of a dork.

But Edith really seemed like she had it all together."

"I wondered about that too," I admitted. Glancing around, I made sure nobody else was close enough to hear our conversation, then leaned forward and lowered my voice. "In fact, I asked Charlie about it before he left the station house, and he told me something interesting. He knew Edith in high school too. The two of them even went out a few times . . . until Charlie caught her cheating on a math test. Apparently, he turned her in to the teacher and told her he couldn't see her anymore." I shrugged and sat back. "So I'm wondering if Edith maybe isn't quite as mature and together as she seemed, you know?"

"Wow." George let out a low whistle. "Talk about holding a grudge . . ."

"I know." I flashed back to the look of pure enmity in Edith's eyes when she'd spotted me in the lobby of the police station earlier that day. "I'm guessing Lionel didn't have to try too hard to talk her into his plan."

"But how was it that she managed to be lurking around when you were in Charlie's house snooping?" Bess asked. "She couldn't possibly have known you'd sneak in just then."

"That was just bad luck, I guess," I said, recalling more of what I'd learned at the police station after Lionel's arrest. "Edith had sneaked back in to make sure her fingerprints weren't anywhere inside—just in case the police came back to check. See, she'd counted on being called over to retrieve the snake when they found it, but it turned out they had an officer with enough experience to do it himself. So while it would have been no surprise if they checked and found her brother's prints in the house, finding hers would've been pretty suspicious."

"So she decides to scare you off with a deadly snake." George shook her head in disgust. "Nice."

"Yeah." I shuddered, thinking back to my close call. "And then she tries it again when I start sniffing around a little too closely at the zoo this morning. That one was a little clumsy—I guess she panicked and tried to get rid of me any way she could."

"Is that how you knew she was involved?" George asked, still leaning back on her elbows.

"Not entirely. I mean, it could have been Bones, too, or any of the other keepers who were around at the time."

"Yeah, what about Bones?" George sat up straight and glanced over at me. "He acted so odd—are you sure he wasn't involved in this too? Maybe helping Edith with the snake or something?"

"I don't think so," Bess responded before I could answer. "I still think he's just sort of nerdy and socially inept, especially when it comes to women."

"I think you're right," I agreed. "I was thinking about what you said about him before, and I realized that he acted even odder whenever Edith was around. Like the way he completely switched his story around when she contradicted him—at the time I thought that was suspicious. But looking back, I think he was just trying to stay on her good side. He probably has a major crush on her."

"Okay. So how *did* you figure out whodunit?" George asked.

"I guess the real turning point was that loose lizard," I said. "But I probably should have figured it out earlier. It was just too much of a coincidence that Edith and Lionel were brother and sister, not to mention Lionel's proficiency in handling that rattlesnake that was after me. How many random people off the street would have known what to do in that situation?"

"I didn't think of that," Bess admitted. "I was just so scared for you, and so relieved when you were safe."

"Me too," I agreed. "At least at first. It was only later that I really thought about it. Lionel kept making it sound like he barely knew anything about Charlie's reptiles, but that kind of gave him away. And once I discovered his relationship to Edith and remembered him complaining about money once or twice, I figured they had to be the culprits." I paused. "It was one of those cases where I mostly figured out what *couldn't* have happened, and then whatever was left was what *did* happen, you know?"

"Yeah," George said. "But the thing is, most people would've thought that the Charlie thing was one that definitely *could* have happened."

"I know. But I believed in him."

George smirked and glanced at Bess. "Isn't that sweet?"

Bess giggled. "I guess that's why he called her during the ride over here."

"It wasn't a big deal." I rolled my eyes, knowing I was lucky that this was the first hint of teasing I'd heard since the call I'd received in the minivan a short while earlier. "He just felt bad that he didn't have a chance to say thanks in all the commotion down at the station. We only talked for a minute, as you know."

"Yeah, that was a surprise," George said. "After what you did for him, I was pretty much expecting him to propose or something."

Bess laughed again, but I just smiled. "Charlie is a quiet, shy, sedate sort of guy," I reminded them. "Why should his thank-you be any different?"

Just then we noticed a commotion down by the pool, where the swimmers from the home team were just starting to gather. "Hey, what's up down there?" George asked, leaning forward to peer down at the milling swimmers. She frowned. "And where's Scott? I don't see him."

Moments later we were pushing our way down through the lower bleachers on our way to see what was happening. We made our way over to the coach . . . only to discover that George's brother was missing yet again!

"But he said he was just stepping outside the locker room for some fresh air, Coach," one of the other boys was saying anxiously.

"Enough is enough!" the coach exclaimed, clutching at his buzz-cut hair. "If Scott Fayne isn't out here and ready to swim in the next fifteen minutes, he's off the team!"

Bess gasped. "We've got to find him!" she cried. "Swimming is his thing—he'll be crushed if he's kicked off the team!"

"He should've thought of that before he started pulling these disappearing acts," George grumbled.

But I was already heading for the locker room. "Come on," I called over my shoulder. "Fifteen minutes isn't much time. We'd better split up and start searching."

Five minutes later I was picking my way across the packed-dirt yard behind the locker room. It was weedy, with scrubby trees and bushes sprouting here and there and piles of empty chlorine bottles and other detritus scattered around. Soon after my friends and I had parted ways to search, I'd noticed the faint imprint of a bare foot in the slightly damp soil just outside the locker room door. That clue had led me out there into the dimly lit yard.

I found Scott sitting next to the chain-link fence at the edge of the lot, staring blankly out toward the brick wall of the building next door. "Hey," I said quietly, crouching down beside him.

He jumped, obviously startled by my sudden appearance. "N-Nancy!" he blurted out. "How did you—what are you . . ."

"Come on." I smiled at him. "You may be able to hide from George and your coach and your parents, but you should know by now that you can't hide from me. I'm the detective, remember?"

He smiled slightly, then frowned. "You're not going to tell them where I am, are you?"

"That depends on why you're out here," I countered. "Are you going to confess right now, or do I have to bring out the interrogation methods I use on hardened criminals?"

This time he barely cracked a smile before letting out a heartfelt sigh. "Whatever," he muttered. "It's not a big deal."

"It's big enough to make you miss practice," I pointed out. "And now you might miss the meet, too, and maybe get kicked off the team. Is that what you want?"

To my surprise, he merely shrugged. "I dunno."

I was starting to realize that there was more than ordinary teenage grumpiness going on here. "Please talk to me, Scott," I urged. "If something's wrong—if your coach is treating you badly, or the other kids are bullying you—"

"No!" Scott looked up, alarmed. "It's nothing like that. It's just me. If I go out there . . ."

"What?" I stared at him. "What are you worried about?"

"If we win this meet, we go to Regionals!" he blurted out. His words, which had been like pulling teeth until now, suddenly came in a flood. "They're counting on me to help get us there, and I don't know if I can do it. Plus if we do make it, there's supposed to be college scouts there watching the older kids, and . . ."

There was more, but by now I'd figured out what was to blame for Scott's mysterious disappearances: nerves. Poor Scott had been worrying over this big meet, putting so much pressure on himself that he was about to explode. He'd all but made himself sick over the thought that his team was counting on him . . . and he might let them down.

"Look," I told him after he'd spit out all his anxiety. "All you can do is your best, right? And so far, when it comes to swimming, your best is pretty darn good."

"I know," he began. "But . . ."

"But nothing. Yeah, you're the star of the team. You earned that place, remember? You did it by showing up at practice, and working hard, and winning races." For a moment I flashed back to Lionel. Unlike Scott, he'd thought he deserved more than he had, rather than worrying that he had more than he deserved. And instead of working for it, he'd tried to take it at the expense of someone else. It was just another reminder that there were all kinds of people in the world—and some of them were pretty misguided.

Meanwhile, Scott still looked worried. "I guess you're right," he mumbled.

I sighed, feeling sorry for him. "Look, if you really aren't having fun anymore, maybe you should quit the team," I said. "Try something else for a while. I'm sure your family would support you if that's really how you feel."

He glanced up at me, looking startled. "But that's not how I feel!" he exclaimed. "I love swimming. I don't want to quit. I just don't want to lose!"

I smiled and patted him on the back, recognizing that the worst had already passed. "Then there's just one thing to do," I told him as I stood up and gestured for him to follow. "Make sure you swim faster than everybody else."

Scott made it back to the pool just in time, and he ended up doing exactly as I'd advised—swimming faster than everybody else, winning all his heats, and clinching the victory for his team. I guess that helped his mood even more than my little pep talk, because by the end of the evening the old, cheerful, likable Scott had returned, much to his family's relief.

As a matter of fact, we were all in a good, almost giddy mood as we headed out of the pool and across the parking lot after the meet. There we found one last surprise.

"Nancy!" Bess exclaimed, elbowing me in the ribs. "Look—isn't that Charlie's tow truck over there?"

I followed her gaze to the green and white truck parked near the exit. My jaw dropped. The entire truck was outlined in flashing, colorful Christmas lights, creating a spectacle that was attracting attention from everyone leaving the meet as well as people driving past on the street. Leaning against the driver's side door, his arms crossed over his chest and a big grin on his face, was Charlie Adams.

I goggled at him, amazed once again by the vagaries of human nature. Because what Charlie was doing was definitely not quiet, shy, or sedate. In addition to the lights outlining the shape of the truck, other, even brighter lights spelled out four words in their blinking, multicolored bulbs:

THANK YOU NANCY DREW!

REDISCOVER THE CLASSIC MYSTERIES OF NANCY DREW

PENDRAGON

Bobby Pendragon is a seemingly normal fourteen-year-old boy. He has a family, a home, and a possible new girlfriend. But something happens to Bobby that changes his life forever.

HE IS CHOSEN TO DETERMINE
THE COURSE OF HUMAN EXISTENCE.

Pulled away from the comfort of his family and suburban home, Bobby is launched into the middle of an immense, interdimensional conflict involving racial tensions, threatened ecosystems, and more. It's a journey of danger and discovery for Bobby, and his success or failure will do nothing less than determine the fate of the world. . . .

PENDRAGON

by D. J. MacHale

Book One: The Merchant of Death
Book Two: The Lost City of Faar
Book Three: The Never War
Book Four: The Reality Bug
Book Five: Black Water

Coming Soon: Book Six: The Rivers of Zadaa

From Aladdin Paperbacks • Published by Simon & Schuster

TOM SWIFT ™
young inventor

He's smart, impossibly cool under pressure, and has more gadgets than he has time for— meet Tom Swift, Young Inventor!

From the creators of Nancy Drew and the Hardy Boys comes a series that's chock-full of adventure, high-tech gadgets, and even higher stakes. Look for a new Tom Swift adventure three times a year!

#1 INTO THE ABYSS
By Victor Appleton

#2 THE ROBOT OLYMPICS
By Victor Appleton

#3 THE SPACE HOTEL
By Victor Appleton